Echo glanced around frantically. She couldn't let him find her here, especially now that she'd savaged his beloved bike.

But there was nowhere to hide.

Eyes wide with terror, Echo scuttled backward, into the darkest depths of the cave, looking for a way out.

There was none. . . .

Terrifying thrillers by Diane Hoh:

Funhouse
The Accident
The Invitation
The Train
The Fever

Nightmare Hall: The Silent Scream
Nightmare Hall: The Roommate
Nightmare Hall: Deadly Attraction
Nightmare Hall: The Wish
Nightmare Hall: The Scream Team
Nightmare Hall: Guilty
Nightmare Hall: Pretty Please
Nightmare Hall: The Experiment
Nightmare Hall: The Night Walker
Nightmare Hall: Sorority Sister
Nightmare Hall: Last Date
Nightmare Hall: The Whisperer
Nightmare Hall: Monster
Nightmare Hall: The Initiation
Nightmare Hall: Truth or Die
Nightmare Hall: Book of Horrors
Nightmare Hall: Last Breath
Nightmare Hall: Win, Lose or Die
Nightmare Hall: The Coffin
Nightmare Hall: Deadly Visions
Nightmare Hall: Student Body
Nightmare Hall: The Vampire's Kiss
Nightmare Hall: Dark Moon
Nightmare Hall: The Biker

NIGHTMARE HALL

The Biker

DIANE HOH

SCHOLASTIC INC.
New York Toronto London Auckland Sydney

ISBN 0-590-25080-9

12 11 10 9 8 7 6 5 4 3 2 1   5 6 7 8 9/9 0/0

Printed in the U.S.A.   01

First Scholastic printing, June 1995

Prologue

The roar of the motorcycle's engine is so loud it can be heard from a great distance on this still, quiet spring night. An elderly woman named Myra pruning her favorite rose bush, the blooms pink with a faint hint of vanilla in their unfolding petals, lifts her head at the sound, and the straw hat she is wearing over her graying hair tilts slightly backward, exposing a lined forehead above slightly puzzled blue eyes.

Two houses up the street in the small, pleasant town of Twin Falls not far from Salem University's campus, the little Johnson boy, just turned seven and proud of it, fights to maintain his balance on the brand-new, shiny red and silver bicycle given him the night before at his birthday celebration. He loves motorcycles, and when he hears the unmistakable roar coming from somewhere behind him, he loses his concentration, then his balance, and topples off the bike. It rolls forward several feet, and then quietly lies down on its side near the curb, as if waiting for the little boy to catch up.

Although he has scraped his knee, drawing blood, the boy is too interested in the possible approach of a real, live motorcycle to cry. He pulls himself to his feet and stands in the middle of the street, eyes bright with anticipation.

It is twilight. The street, its neat white or brick houses and the fully leafed, large trees lining the avenue, are all bathed in faint purple shadows as darkness begins to silently swallow Twin Falls, gobbling it up block by block.

Any vehicle on the road at this hour is required to turn on its lights. That is the law.

But, though the roar of the bike increases in volume and intensity, the woman tending her roses and the little boy in the street see no sign of a light approaching.

If he had seen a light, the little Johnson boy would have moved out of the street and onto the curb to watch the motorcycle fly by, and would have counted himself lucky to see such a sight.

Myra, puzzled by the loud roar of the motorcycle when she can see no sign of the vehicle itself, rises to her feet and steps out into the street to peer down the avenue, thinking per-

haps the roar isn't that of a motorcycle, after all, but someone's power lawnmower. She has seen the little Johnson boy in the street trying to ride his new bicycle, and wonders if she should call to him to move to the curb, just in case. But his parents might not like that, might think she's just being nosy.

She does see a light then, but it's confusing, because it's a double set of headlights, coming toward her end of the street. She may be old, but she knows perfectly well that motorcycles don't have two headlights.

Then what is that dreadful roar, so loud it could easily finish off what's left of her hearing?

The cycle appears out of nowhere, only slightly illuminated by the headlights of the car still some distance behind it. It is a huge Harley-Davidson with, it's true, no headlight at all, and only one rider. It swoops with a roar out of the purple shadows, catching the little Johnson boy by surprise. He wavers, his eyes widening in astonishment, and then that amazing self-protective instinct kicks in and he dives sideways, out of the path of the on-coming motorcycle.

But the boy misjudges the distance between street and curb and, as the rose-tending woman up the street watches in horror, the little John-son boy misses the grassy area just beyond the curb, and falls too soon, his head slamming into the cement curb with a deadly thwacking sound.

Then there are three more sounds, each one breaking the early evening silence in a different way. There is the triumphant roar of the motorcycle as it races away. There is the shrill scream of Myra as she rushes across the street to aid the injured boy, and then the agonized shriek of brakes as the approaching car tries desperately to avoid hitting her.

It fails.

The sound when the car hits her is quieter than the earlier sound of the boy's head thwacking into the curb. It is a softer noise, almost gentle as the sedan with the shrieking brakes collides with the woman, knocking her backward and under the car. It keeps going for a few more feet, dragging its victim along with it. When the car finally slides to a complete halt, the hem of a blue denim skirt clings to the bottom of the left front wheel.

Hearing the odd assortment of sounds from inside his house, the woman's husband rises from his leather recliner in front of the television set and hurries to the front door, opening it and calling, "Myra? Myra?"

The little Johnson boy lies perfectly still, his legs limp in the street, his head on the curb. A small pool of bright red, looking very like the round shiny red apples he often drew in first grade, forms beneath his skull.

Still, he will survive and go into second grade in September.

But Myra's pink and vanilla tinted roses will have to be pruned by someone else if they are to retain their customary glory. As the coroner tells her grief-stricken husband later, "She was dead before she hit the ground. Heart attack. Sorry, Milt."

The Twin Falls police will hunt for the Harley-Davidson. But, as one of the officers on the scene tells the grieving Milt, "Far as we know, the biker isn't guilty of much. He didn't hit anyone. Wasn't speeding, according to witnesses. They said the bike didn't have a light on, and we could ticket him for that, if we find him. But we're sure not gonna hang him for that."

Alone in her room on the campus of Salem University, Echo Glenn hears the roar of a motorcycle as it approaches campus and thinks, What a racket!

Then she returns to her studying.

Chapter 1

"Well, I don't care what anyone says, I think it's scary," Delores Jean Cutter said. Immersed to her neck in the bubbling whirlpool in Salem University's infirmary, she shook her head. Dark, short hair curled damply around her pink cheeks. "I mean, that little boy could have been killed. And that old woman *was*. All because of some idiot on a motorcycle! Echo, could you please hand me another towel? This one's soggy."

"That's because you've been waving it around, too close to the whirlpool bubbles, while you were talking, Deejay," Echo said. But she got up from the stool where she'd been sitting with an open book in her lap, took a thick, white towel from the tall, wide supply closet and slung it carelessly around Deejay's shoulders. Her part-time job at the infirmary required her to see that the people who used the whirlpool had what they needed. Sometimes she felt like an attendant at a country club, but the job brought in needed funds. Beggars couldn't be choosers. "The article in the campus paper said the biker didn't do anything wrong except forget to turn his light on. He didn't hit that woman or the little boy."

Deejay Cutter slapped at the whirling water with the flat of her hand and said emphatically, "But it wouldn't have happened if the motorcycle had had its light on, Echo!" The other two girls in the whirlpool all nodded agreement. "And why are you defending the guy, anyway?"

Echo had no idea why she was taking the side of the biker. She didn't even know who he was. No one did.

"Well, at least the attack happened in town," Ruthanne Widdoes said, standing up and stepping stiffly out of the tub. Ruthanne had arthritis, a painful disease unusual in someone so young, and spent more time than anyone else in the whirlpool. She was very tall and thin and had told Echo that her pediatrician had said she'd "grown too fast." "He made it sound like it was my fault," she had complained to Echo one day as she stepped gingerly into the tub. "Like I did it on purpose." Now, Ruthanne added, "It's not like there's a wild biker loose right here on campus."

Echo didn't say anything, but she was remembering the sound she'd heard the night before when she was studying. The unmistakable roar of a motorcycle's engine arriving on campus. But that didn't mean anything. There *were* a few bikes on campus. They were cheaper to run and easier to maneuver in traffic than a car.

"Well, I just hope he *stays* in town," Deejay said. "I don't like motorcycles. Too noisy." Deejay's problem was tennis elbow. Still athletically inclined, she had switched to swimming, saying it was a form of "hydrotherapy," like the whirlpool, only not as warm and bubbly.

Marilyn Sexton nodded agreement. Tall and blonde and as shy and quiet as Deejay was talkative, Marilyn had what Echo thought of as "sad eyes." The victim of a tragic house fire when she was a teenager, her legs and arms not only pained her from time to time, they were badly scarred. Marilyn never wore shorts or tops without long sleeves. Echo was certain that only Marilyn's roommate and her whirlpool room companions had ever seen Marilyn's cruel scars.

The three girls were very different. Deejay

was popular and outgoing, Marilyn shy and quiet, Ruthanne a little brusque but very capable and efficient. In spite of her pain, Ruthanne accomplished a lot on campus, heading fund raisers, chairing committees, and making the dean's list. The three seemed to have little in common. Echo was sure they would never have become friends if not for their shared need for the whirlpool's soothing waters.

Echo tolerated the trio, but she didn't consider them close friends. She had no close friends. Her choice.

"Are you going to the picnic tomorrow afternoon, Echo?" Marilyn asked as she climbed out of the tub.

"No." Picnic? An entire Saturday afternoon spent in the hot sun, with ants nibbling at her ankles and people throwing water balloons at each other? No, thanks.

"You're so antisocial, Echo," Ruthanne accused as she towelled off her long, skinny legs. "You really don't like people, do you?"

"That's not true!" Echo protested halfheartedly. But she knew it was almost true. She wasn't even sure she liked these three, although she had talked to them more this year than to anyone else on campus. But that was solely because of her job at the infirmary. She spent almost no time with them away from the whirlpool room. It's not that they were that bad; Deejay was fun, Marilyn was nice enough, and Ruthanne, when she wasn't complaining about pain, could carry on a very intelligent conversation.

But they had all been handed their educations on a silver platter. None of the three worked part-time to help out with expenses. They actually got "allowances" in the mail from their parents, money they were free to spend as they liked. And they all had parents who had shown up on Parents' Day.

No one had ever taken the time or energy to spoil Echo Glenn, that was what it came down to. She was jealous. So how could she possibly like them?

Besides, they were all so wrapped up in themselves. If any one of the three had ever taken the time to ask her how *she* was, how she was feeling and what she was thinking, the thick, curly hair on her head, the same color as the burnt sienna crayon in a Crayola box, would have turned white with shock.

"I guess I'm not surprised that you defended that biker," Ruthanne continued as she dressed. "You're sort of the type." She wasn't accusing, she was just stating what she saw as fact. "Always trying to stir things up. I wouldn't be at all surprised to see you sporting a black leather jacket and boots any day now."

"Stuff it, Ruthanne," Echo said bluntly. She knew exactly what Ruthanne was referring to. That business about trying to get more girls' restrooms installed at the stadium. At every game, there were long lines of waiting females. Echo had missed some really spectacular plays standing in line. So she'd gone public with her complaint. So what? It hadn't done any good, but she'd felt better because at least she'd done something: circulating a petition, denouncing the administration's lack of response to that petition from the steps of the library. I wasn't trying to be different, she thought defensively, I was just trying to accomplish something useful, that's all. Everyone's so apathetic. No one wants to rock the boat. As long as Ruthanne has a date for Friday and Saturday nights, and probably Sunday, too, she couldn't care less if she has to stand on line until her teeth fall out.

"We *need* those restrooms," she said as she carried the wet towels to the hamper.

"Oh, and I suppose we really needed that brouhaha you started over poor lighting in the main parking lot, too," Marilyn said as she earnestly wrestled with her ponytail, to make the ends curl under exactly right.

"It's dark in that lot," Echo said mildly. She never wasted energy getting angry at these three. She didn't care enough about them for that. "If a mad biker came at you in that lot, you wouldn't see him until he was right on top of you."

The ponytail having done her bidding, Marilyn smiled sweetly. "Oh, Echo, there's no mad biker on campus. And there wasn't even one in town when you started that fuss about the parking lot. You just wanted to stir up trouble, that's all. Admit it!"

"If you guys are done," Echo bit off one word at a time, "you can leave. I can't sit here all day talking. *I've* got work to do." Unlike some of us, she thought.

"So you're not coming to the picnic?" Ruthanne asked when she had dressed in a pink sweatsuit and slicked her long, blonde hair away from her face. Echo noticed with satisfaction that she wasn't limping as noticeably. The whirlpool always helped.

"No, I am not going to any picnic."

"But you're coming to the mall with me later, right?" Deejay asked. "You promised."

Echo had only promised because Deejay had said Marilyn and Ruthanne both had dates and Deejay hated going to the mall alone. Deejay never did anything alone. Seldom had to. If Echo went by herself, she'd be in and out in five minutes. Going with Deejay could mean hours. But she'd promised. "I guess. I need shampoo, and it's too expensive at the bookstore. Meet you out front at seven, when I finish here. But I'm *not* hanging out in that mall all night, Deejay! I have better things to do."

Deejay laughed. "Oh, Echo, everyone's right about you. You *are* antisocial. You're hopeless."

After she left, Echo folded towels and thought about that. Antisocial? Maybe. The thing was, Echo Glenn had no desire to be close to anyone. You could get hurt that way. And she didn't want to be hurt anymore.

She had had a family, once, just like everybody else. A mom, a dad, a dog Spot. Well, actually, the dog's name was Picardy, but he was every bit as cute as the little dog in those stupid first-grade books about families. Then her parents had divorced. That happened when she was twelve, and needed a strong, solid family more than ever. Her father remarried almost immediately, moved to California, and began a new family. She hadn't seen him in years, although he sent a small check every Christmas and another check two weeks after her birthday because he always forgot the date.

Her mother had remarried a year later. A military man who moved around a lot. She left

Echo with her own elderly parents. "A child needs to stay in one place," she had reasoned.

Well, no, not really. What a child needs is a family.

Echo hadn't seen her mother since she was fourteen, and now had no desire to. She also had two "new" children. She wasn't even sure she would recognize her.

Her grandparents had been good to her. But they were old now, and wrapped up in each other's ailments. Before he retired, her grandfather had been a lawyer, but not a very good one. Never made much money, which left Echo responsible for her own higher education.

She had no plans to return to her grandparents' house for summer vacations or holidays. They probably wouldn't even notice that she wasn't there.

All she wanted to do now was get an excellent education, no matter what it took, and become a lawyer and consumer advocate. Then she could always, always take care of herself and would never need anyone else to do it for her.

The trouble with counting on someone else taking care of you, it seemed to her, was that they might not always be there for you. And then what would you do?

Cry a lot.

That would never, never happen to her again.

Deejay was okay. But Echo would never consider making Deejay her best friend. She hadn't had one since she was twelve. Twelve-and-a-half, actually. That was when her mother took her out of school, away from the friends and neighborhood she'd known all of her life and shipped her to her grandparents in Jamestown, New York, so that Stella Glenn's precious military man wouldn't leave her behind. It hadn't seemed to matter to anyone that Echo was leaving her own best friend, Geneva Teresa Scalise, someone she'd known since second grade, behind.

They had written for a while, called each other on Christmas the first year. Then, nothing. Nothing at all, teaching Echo that absence did *not* necessarily make the heart grow fonder, after all. Geneva, Echo had heard last year, married her high school boyfriend the day after graduation. He'd enlisted in the service, and they had moved to Germany.

Full circle, Echo thought bitterly as she picked up her shoulder bag, closed the door to the whirlpool room and locked it, dropping the key on the nurse's desk.

Deejay was sitting on the curb outside the infirmary, talking to a tall, good-looking boy in jeans and a cutoff T-shirt. He looked vaguely familiar, but turned and loped away before Echo reached the pair.

"Who was that?" she asked, thinking that she'd seen the guy before.

Deejay stood up, dusting off the seat of her jeans. "Liam McCullough. You know him, don't you? He's really nice."

"I've run into him on campus," Echo said dryly as they headed for the shuttle bus stop, and didn't elaborate further. She meant it literally. She *had* run into McCullough, on one of the first really warm days in May. She'd been riding her bike, too fast as always, along the river path behind campus and, lost in the beauty of the day and the rushing of the sun-streaked river, hadn't seen anyone coming.

He'd let out a husky "Oof!" when she hit him broadside as he emerged onto the path from the woods. And then he'd stumbled backward and landed on his back on the grass. Hadn't been hurt, except for a bruised ego. But he'd certainly been mad, his eyes flashing as he stood up, brushed himself off and shouted at her, "Why don't you watch where you're going?"

Honestly, you'd have thought she'd done it on purpose! And why hadn't *he* been watching where he was going?

Unfortunately, a campus traffic policeman had just happened to be coming from the opposite direction, and had witnessed the accident. Just her luck. She got a ticket, had to pay a fifteen-dollar fine. Not good news when you only have a part-time job at the infirmary, which pays next to nothing.

She hadn't even told the victim good-bye when, ticket in hand, she pedalled away from the scene. And she hadn't seen him since.

Maybe he *was* nice. But he sure could yell.

It was early on Friday evening. Echo knew the mall would be crowded until later when everyone abandoned shopping for the more interesting pursuits of parties and dances and movies and dancing at some nightclub in town. If that was how they wanted to spend their time, that was fine with her. As long as no one insisted that she waste *her* time that way, too.

Deejay had tried. "Echo, you're supposed to be having *fun* at college. I never see you having any fun!"

"I'm supposed to be getting an education," Echo had snapped, "and that's what I'm doing!"

She stayed very busy, studying, reading, working at the infirmary. Often, she felt bored and restless. She didn't call it loneliness, because that would have meant she needed people, and that thought revolted her. She wasn't lonely or needy. She was *not*.

But sometimes, she couldn't sleep at night and got up after her roommate, Trixie, was asleep, no doubt dreaming of boys with big muscles and tiny brains because that was who Trixie *was*, and went walking alone along the river. She sometimes wondered, on those solitary outings, how both of her parents had been able and willing to shut their own daughter out of their lives so easily, but she pushed the thought away quickly, before it could take hold like a nasty bee sinking its stinger into her skin.

Anyway, it didn't matter. Not anymore. She was doing fine, thank you very much, and didn't need anyone. She could take care of herself. She had been doing just that for a long time now, and would continue to.

Echo couldn't imagine any situation that she might not be able to handle by herself. So far, there hadn't been one. So far, she'd been lucky.

She bought shampoo, accompanied by Deejay's laughing complaints about how Echo took forever to sort through all of the bottles until she found the cheapest brand.

They looked at the new summer clothing and after a brief argument with herself, Echo returned to the rack a really pretty, white slip dress that would be perfect for summer.

"You should get it," Deejay urged. "It's on sale, Echo. You're tall and thin enough to wear a dress like that. It'd look great."

"I don't have any place to wear it." She'd be working full-time this summer at the library in town and probably could spring for the dress. She was getting awfully tired of being sensible all the time. But she really *didn't* have any place to wear something so pretty.

Back on the rack it went.

But she couldn't help casting one last, yearning glance over her shoulder as they left the store.

Because Deejay had a party to attend, which Echo had no intention of attending, they parted at the food court after a quick sandwich.

Reluctant to return to an empty dorm room on a Friday night, Echo spent an hour or so browsing in the bookstore until she felt tired enough to go back to campus.

The mall was emptying out fast.

A crowd had gathered under the canopy outside. Some were waiting for the local bus, some for the shuttle, some just spending a few extra minutes talking about evening plans before actually fulfilling them.

Echo heard the roar before anyone else did. She had moved away from the crowd, up to the curb at the end of the walkway, and was far enough away from the crowd's noise to hear the unmistakable sound of a motorcycle's engine. Later, she would remember thinking how much it sounded like the bellow of a wild animal.

Minutes later, the comparison would seem painfully appropriate, as the motorcycle, its light shining in the evening darkness, raced through the parking lot and up over the curb fifty yards or so from where Echo was standing. It headed straight for the crowd.

There was one long moment when people realized something was happening but weren't sure what, and then the awful truth sank in. With it came panic.

Screams and shouts rang out as people bolted, scrambling frantically to escape the roaring machine.

Some took refuge behind the stone benches that lined the cement walkway under the canopy. Others dove into the tall, full bushes beside the benches. One skinny, blond guy in jeans and a denim jacket attempted to make it to the mall's big, glass double doors, but he tripped over someone's feet and fell. His head slammed into the solid metal door frame. His body went limp, effectively blocking the door from opening from the inside.

The bike spun in circles, teasing, tantalizing,

as people continued to slam into each other in an attempt to find safety.

Two girls began, at the exact same moment, to run in the same direction and knocked right into each other.

Echo waited breathlessly for the motorcycle to run over the fallen girls.

It didn't. But it raced its engine threateningly until both girls scrambled to their feet and rushed to the protection of one of the bushes.

Echo, far enough away to feel relatively safe, studied the figure on the bike. It was dressed from head to toe in black leather, its hair hidden by a shiny black helmet, its face a mystery behind a thick plastic shield.

The bike revved its motor with triumph and was already turning away when Echo corrected her first impression. He *wasn't* dressed from head to toe in black leather. Not entirely. The boots were not black leather.

The boots were, in fact, very colorful. They boasted a black background with a striking diamond design in deep wine and forest green running up the side. Snakeskin, Echo thought.

As the bike turned and raced away, she couldn't help but notice a tiny, silver figure of a genie's lamp dangling from a silver chain fastened around the instep of the boot facing her.

Interesting. The boots were unusual. Distinctive.

But not that unusual. Because Echo had seen a pair exactly like them somewhere else.

What was even more interesting was, she remembered where she had seen them.

And most interesting of all, she remembered *who* had been wearing them.

Chapter 2

Although the crowd under the mall canopy was incensed by the reckless action of the biker, the two mall security officers who arrived after the bike had roared away from the scene were at a loss. One shrugged and said, "You didn't get the license plate, we got nothing to go on," and the other asked a shaken victim, "Can't you remember *anything* unusual about the guy? A scar on his face, a tattoo, something?"

Echo knew this was the moment to speak up. How many pair of boots like that could there be in the university area? They'd looked custom-designed, or at least special-ordered, not the kind of boot you saw in an ordinary store window. Even if her eyes had tricked her and the diamond design on the pair she'd just seen was in different shades of green and wine than the pair she had seen at school, she could at least give the police the name of the person she now suspected, and leave it to them to check things out.

That was certainly what she should do.

But her tongue clung to the roof of her mouth, held captive there because she was unwilling to set it free. She told herself stubbornly that he hadn't hurt anyone, not really. They'd hurt themselves, panicking like horses in a burning barn. Was that *his* fault?

Well, yes, of course it was his fault, for scaring them in the first place. What was he up to, anyway? What satisfaction did he get out of aiming that huge, deadly machine at a crowd of people? The only reason someone *hadn't* been killed or maimed was his expertise in handling the bike. Amazing, the way he sped in and out, making dizzying turns, missing his victims by no more than a hair-raising millimeter. He could probably turn that thing on a dime.

But the person she'd seen the boots on at school . . . couldn't be the person who'd been on that bike. Couldn't possibly. She tried to imagine that person racing on a roaring bike into a crowd of people, deliberately aiming straight at them, and almost laughed aloud. Right. That was about as likely as her showing up at a sorority party. Never happen.

So she held her tongue. No mention of the unique boots passed her lips. She would talk to him first, hunt him down and confront him. After all, she couldn't fling accusations around like confetti until she had more to go on. Maybe she'd be able to tell when she talked to him if she was way off base. And if she was right and he admitted it, maybe she'd find out the *why* of it.

She did like to know the *why* of things, although it seemed to her that she seldom got the chance. There were a million things she'd never learned the why of, and not just why her parents had dumped her. There were plenty of other things. Some were trivial, like why every other girl at school ranked the importance of their makeup right up there with three meals a day. Some things, though, were more important, like why it was so crucial for everyone to be the same. To dress the same, talk the same, behave in the same way. If you insisted on being different in any of those areas (and a few others), you were shoved into a box labelled "Not One of Us" or and you stayed in that box until you saw the error of your ways, repented, and became like everyone else.

Why *was* that?

Echo had thought that college would be different. Had hoped, had prayed, that it would be.

But it wasn't. Not really. She knew a girl

named Johanna, a really pretty girl who was also smart and funny, who had been popular at the beginning of the year. Then, halfway through first semester, she had pierced her nose and hung a tiny gold ring in one nostril.

Presto chango! Into the "Different" box she went. And as far as Echo knew, there she stayed.

And there was that boy in her psych class. John Dover. He was short and very, very overweight. She had heard people calling him "Double-Dover." In class, at his desk, his body hung over the seat like a soufflé baked in a too-small dish.

He, of course, had gone into the box on the very first day of school. But then, he'd probably been in that same box all through high school and was used to it. Probably hadn't expected anything else of college.

"Regular" people on campus didn't wear boots like the ones she'd seen on the biker. Ever. They wore pretty, heeled boots with skirts and dresses, and ankle boots with jeans. But "regular" people at Salem U. didn't wear high-heeled cowboy boots made of snakeskin with wine and green diamonds running up the sides and a silver chain fastened around the instep.

Was the person on whom she had seen those

boots in class "different" enough to climb on a motorcycle? She wasn't sure. He wasn't very popular. But he was in a fraternity, and Deejay, Marilyn, and Ruthanne all knew him. That didn't mean they liked him, though. Maybe he was as much of an outsider as she herself was.

But she just couldn't picture him in black leather, racing a motorcycle into a crowd.

Still, Echo thought as she climbed aboard the small, yellow shuttle bus with a group of very shaken, frightened people glad to be out from under the mall canopy, you just could never tell about people. Could you?

His name was Pruitt. Aaron Pruitt. He was in her psych class. He was tall, and thin, and pale-faced, even this late in the spring. His sandy hair was cut short, precisely parted in the middle and neatly plastered flat with gel, except for the cowlick at the crown, which could probably only be subdued with a hefty application of glue. His glasses were wire-rimmed and he had a nice, straight nose to sit the glasses on. But he was basically an unsmiling, silent creature.

Maybe he didn't have anything to smile about, Echo thought.

He was always neatly dressed. His long-sleeved shirts were perfectly pressed and always tucked in, never without a belt. He didn't wear jeans, although he had, she was sure, been wearing them last night. Maybe you had to wear jeans on a motorcycle. Even his backpack, she had noticed once in class, was always clean. It was a navy blue canvas affair that looked expensive and was completely free of grease spots and loosely flapping papers and slashes of black or blue or red from felt-tipped pens.

Pruitt?

Nah.

In psych class, she sat behind him and over one row, which was how she'd come to notice the boots. He always slid down in his seat as far as possible without actually lying down, and most often, stuck his long, skinny legs out into the aisle, sometimes propping his feet up on the seat opposite his, even if it was occupied. If a guy was sitting in the seat, the guy might not care, might just ignore the feet at the edge of the seat. But the girls who sat there gave the boots a contemptuous push, sending the skinny legs to the floor with a thunk.

Remembering the expression of cold contempt on Pruitt's face when a girl did that, Echo could almost imagine him racing into the crowd at the mall on a roaring motorcycle.

Almost. But not quite.

She began to feel glad that she hadn't gone

to the police. She'd have felt like a total fool giving them the name of someone like Pruitt in connection with the bizarre attacks. When they first laid eyes on him, they'd have thought she was nuts.

That look she'd seen on Pruitt's face probably just meant that he had little patience with people. That was something they had in common. So maybe she *wasn't* crazy. Maybe, like her, he sometimes got bored and restless. If he *was* the biker, maybe, also like her, he just craved a little adventure.

I could stand a little adventure, too, Echo thought as the shuttle made the sharp left turn onto campus. And he really *hadn't* hurt anyone. It *was* awful that people had been hurt, but that wasn't his fault.

Maybe Pruitt, if that's who it was, wouldn't mind sharing the fun.

The first thing she had to do was make sure she had the right guy.

By morning, Echo had convinced herself that she was being ridiculous. Pruitt couldn't possibly be the biker. The boots had to be a bizarre coincidence, that was all.

Glad she hadn't made the mistake of confronting him, she put the whole nasty business out of her mind and, after attending her Saturday morning classes, went to work at the infirmary.

The whirlpool was empty because of the university picnic.

Echo settled into a corner of the whirlpool room and started cramming for finals, stopping only occasionally when a picnic-goer came in with a bee sting or a bug bite.

When she left the infirmary, the picnic-goers were just beginning to return to campus. Carloads of people were pulling up in front of Lester and Devereaux dorms and letting their occupants spill out, sunburned and laughing.

For just one small moment, Echo felt a painful tug of regret. They *did* look like they'd had fun. And she *had* been invited.

But in the next few seconds, all thoughts of a picnic she might have attended if she weren't so "antisocial" were erased from her mind as the ear-splitting roar of a motorcycle's engine filled the air.

At first, Echo assumed someone had ridden a bike to the picnic and was returning to campus with everyone else.

Then someone screamed. That was quickly followed by another scream. Then a chorus of terrified shouts rose above the grumbling of the bike's motor.

Just like at the mall last night, Echo thought with alarm, and broke into a run.

She arrived on the Commons, a wide area of green grass bordering the parking lot, to find chaos. The scene was so similar to last night's, she felt dizzy with déjà vu. People were running and scrambling to get out of the way of the maniacal motorcycle, shouting and screaming, stumbling over one another in their panic, like victims in a Godzilla movie.

The bike veered in and out, slowing to a crawl, then revving its engine and racing off again into another small group of white-faced picnickers.

He hit no one. But Echo saw one girl, in her rush to escape, fall forward and slam her right arm into a large boulder fronting a bed of flowers.

A boy Echo knew from psych class, looking over his shoulder in fear at the bike as he ran, crashed straight into a red fire hydrant and yelled out in pain when his kneecap took a powerful blow. His other knee caved, and he went down.

Knowing there was nothing she could do for the victims until the motorcycle left, Echo concentrated her attention instead on the biker. He was wearing the boots again. She moved to one side slightly to get a better view. Was he the same size as Aaron Pruitt? Maybe. The black leather jacket could be providing more bulk than Pruitt had. The helmet and face shield made it impossible to distinguish any facial features, but there did seem to be something familiar about the way he was sitting on the bike.

Before she could get closer, the bike veered suddenly and raced away, leaving a dozen or more people sprawled on the grass, dotting the Commons like snow angels.

He *still* hasn't actually hurt anyone with the bike, Echo thought as she hurried to the boy from her psych class. It's pretty mean, scaring people half to death, but it's not *his* fault they're all so clumsy.

In the bedlam that followed, she made up her mind to find Pruitt and confront him. While she helped take the injured to the infirmary, she told herself that if it wasn't him, she'd forget about the whole thing.

But if it *was* him, she thought, as she handed a nurse fresh towels, she wanted to know why he was doing this. And . . . while she was finding out, she just might ask for a ride. Not one that involved scaring the life out of people, of course. She wasn't interested in accompanying him on one of his terrorist attacks. But a regular ride, with the wind blowing in her face and hair as they flew along the highway, could be a lot of fun.

Echo Glenn could use a little fun in her life.

Chapter 3

When things on campus had calmed down and she'd been dismissed from the infirmary, Echo went looking for Pruitt.

She found him in a dark corner at the back of the library, reading. He was reclining in a wooden chair with thick, dark arms. His legs and feet dangled over one arm, while his upper body reclined against the opposite arm. He was wearing khaki pants and a plaid short-sleeved shirt.

And he was wearing the snakeskin boots.

Echo peered more closely at the boots. The shades of wine and green weaving their way up the sides were not lighter or darker than the diamonds she'd noticed the night before and again just a few hours earlier. They were exactly the same colors.

But staring at Pruitt in the chair, his head down, the cowlick sticking up like a flag, she found it nearly impossible to believe that just a little while ago he'd been terrorizing a part of campus on his motorcycle.

Still, there were the boots . . .

She took a seat beside his chair. "Hello, Pruitt," she said, smiling. "Echo Glenn. Monday, Wednesday, Friday, nine o'clock psych."

"I know who you are," he said coolly, not taking his eyes off the book in his lap. "The question is, what do you want?"

Nothing like getting right to the point. Good. That meant he wasn't a game-player, like so many others on campus. She wouldn't play any stupid games, either. "I was wondering if you'd like some company on your next bike ride."

If she had expected his head to shoot up guiltily, she was disappointed. He kept his eyes behind the wire-rimmed glasses fixed on the page in front of him. "Bike ride? Boy, have you got a wrong number! I haven't been on a bike since my sophomore year of high school."

That didn't surprise her. That was probably the year he'd switched to motorcycles. Someone who could handle that Harley as expertly as he did had to have been riding it for a long time. "Not bicycle, Pruitt. Motorcycle. I want to go along the next time you take it out." She grinned. "But you have to promise not to ram it into any crowds while I'm with you."

He did lift his head then, fixing pale eyes on her. He laughed without mirth. "Do I look like a biker to you?"

Echo laughed, too. "No. That's what's so perfect about it. It makes so much sense to me now that I think about it. No one on campus would ever suspect you of being the Mad Biker. That *is* what they're calling you, you know. But," she waggled a finger at him, "I noticed the boots. First in class, when you put your feet up on Marilyn's desk, and then I noticed them at the mall, and again this afternoon when you panicked those students at the Commons. Those are pretty special boots, Pruitt. I couldn't possibly be wrong about them."

He lifted a leg and waved one foot. "They're just boots."

"No, I don't *think* so. They are very unusual boots. But they're just a part of it. A part of the whole package. The Harley, all that black leather, even a face shield so no one will recognize you, those things are the rest of the package. And that package is having a lot more fun than I am, Pruitt. I want to see what it feels like to fly down the highway on the back of a Harley. You can help me do that. After all," Echo added slyly, "I'm doing you a favor, right? I mean, I haven't yet gone to the police or the administration and told them about the boots."

"Like they'd believe *you*," he said flatly. He lifted his head again. "Take a good look at me, Echo. Do you actually *know* anyone who would take you seriously if you accused me of being the Mad Biker? Or *any* biker, for that matter."

Echo shrugged. "Maybe not. But I would at least make them *think* about the possibility, and that would spoil all your fun, wouldn't it? I mean, once the suspicion had been raised, you wouldn't dare climb on that motorcycle again, not for a long time. That would be really stupid, and I don't think you're stupid, are you, Pruitt?"

"You don't?" Now he looked interested. "I didn't know you thought about me at all." He paused, then added. "You don't look like the biker type any more than I do."

"I've never been on a motorcycle in my life," she said. "Never even thought about it until I saw you riding yours. Of course, I didn't know at first that it was you. And I have to admit, you would never have been on my list of possibles." She leaned forward, closer to him, and lowered her voice, although their dim little corner was deserted. "Is that why you're doing it?

Because it's something no one would ever, ever suspect you of doing?"

He sat up, plunking his booted feet down on the hardwood floor. "Never mind about me. I'm more interested in why *you're* here."

"I told you. I just want a ride, that's all. When I saw the way you handled that bike last night, well, it just looked like so much fun. I mean," Echo amended hastily, "not the part about scaring people to death, making them fall all over each other. That's pretty mean if you ask me."

"I didn't."

"But just a ride, maybe to town and back. I don't know anyone with a motorcycle, so you're it."

"Oh, I get it," he said. "You *want* something from me. You haven't spoken to me in class all year, not so much as a hello, and now you suddenly find me fascinating? Because of a motorcycle? What is it about the bike that intrigues you? The noise? The power? The strength? Tell me. I'd like to know."

Echo felt her cheeks burning. He had a point. She hadn't ever spoken to him, and even now, it wasn't him she was interested in, it was the bike ride.

"Aren't you scared?" he persisted, his eyes

still on her face. "You said that what I did last night and today, scaring those people, was mean. So why aren't you afraid of me? How do you know I won't do something really horrible to the one person on campus who's guessed the truth? You've got nerve, I'll say that. Hunting me down and blackmailing me into giving you a ride. Pretty risky, Glenn."

Echo bristled. "I'm *not* blackmailing you! I'm just asking for a favor. One tiny little ride, that's all. Why can't I come with you?"

"Because you might tell, afterward."

She shook her head. "I wouldn't. If I were going to, I'd already have gone to the administration or the cops and told them about the boots. Anyway, it's not like you've killed anyone. You're just scaring them. Is that a crime? Besides, you said yourself no one would believe me. They'd believe you over me any day, right?"

He shook his head doubtfully. "I don't know. Seems risky to me, taking on a passenger. I've been doing just fine on my own. Everyone says you're trouble. I don't want you screwing things up."

"I won't! Just one ride, that's all. I promise I'll disappear then, and I won't say anything to anyone. You don't have to worry about that."

"Oh, I wasn't worried about that," he said, smiling slightly. It was a smile without warmth. He stood up, looking down on her with cool, pale eyes. "Because like me, you're not stupid. You're too smart to do something as dumb as telling on me. That would be the worst thing you could ever do. The *worst*, Echo."

The way he said that made Echo's teeth ache, and she realized she was clenching them. It occurred to her in that moment that she might have made a really bad mistake.

She didn't unclench her teeth until Pruitt said, "I'll think about it. No promises. Call you," and walked away, with a new and arrogant swagger that she didn't think he'd had before. Maybe she'd just never noticed it. After all, as he'd pointed out, she'd never noticed *him* before. Not until last night.

It was easy to figure out why he'd taken to riding a motorcycle. Because the bike was all the things Pruitt wanted to be, but wasn't. Strong. Powerful. Attention-getting. The roar of the engine must especially please him, because he himself was so quiet. Even when he'd been indignant with her, even when he'd threatened her (and she had not the slightest doubt that she *had* been threatened), his voice hadn't risen. No wonder he needed a little noise in his life.

I guess, Echo thought as she picked up her books and left the library, I'd better not plan on any lengthy, detailed conversations with him if he takes me for a ride. Between the sound of the engine roaring and the wind whistling around us, it will be impossible for me to hear such a quiet voice.

So who needed to talk, anyway?

Her heart skipping a beat every now and then when she thought about racing down the highway with the wind in her face, and thought about feeling free and daring and adventurous, Echo went back to Lester to wait for Pruitt's call.

Chapter 4

Echo hadn't the slightest idea whether or not Pruitt would call, but during the hour in her room before she had to go on duty at the infirmary, she stayed as close to the phone as it was humanly possible to get. She only left once, to race downstairs to the vending machine for a sandwich and coffee.

"You're expecting a call?" Trixie asked with as much disbelief in her voice as if she'd asked, "You're expecting to be crowned Miss America?"

"Hard to believe, isn't it?" Echo answered drily. "But yes, I am expecting a call. So I'd appreciate it if you wouldn't keep the phone permanently attached to your ear for a change."

Trixie tossed her long, carefully curled blonde hair and said with disdain, "It's Saturday *night*, Echo. *I'm* not going to be here. So there won't be anyone distracting you from waiting for your little phone call."

Echo laughed. Trixie hadn't said, "from *answering* your phone call." Because Trixie didn't believe the anticipated call would ever come.

Echo wasn't sure she believed it, either. Had she been convincing enough when she'd promised Pruitt that she wouldn't tell?

She ate her sandwich, drank her coffee, and lay down on the bed, not sleeping, not thinking, just waiting and hoping the phone would ring. She *wanted* that bike ride!

Still, when the phone did ring, she jumped, startled.

It was Pruitt. "No way am I coming to your dorm," he said abruptly. "That'd be stupid. Meet me behind the infirmary, near the stone wall. Nine o'clock. If you're not there, I'm taking off." He hung up.

Echo laughed aloud. The guy knew absolutely nothing about making polite, idle conversation. But then, it wasn't her strong suit, either. And she *was* going to get her ride.

First, she had an hour shift at the infirmary. Good. It would make the time go by faster. If she had to stay in her room until nine o'clock, she'd jump out of her skin.

Deejay, Marilyn, and Ruthanne were already in the whirlpool, comfortably settled, when Echo arrived. They were deep in conversation about the two biker attacks.

"I don't understand why no one has apprehended him yet," Ruthanne complained.

Echo had to hide a smile. Apprehended? Ruthanne was an English major.

"Me, either," Marilyn agreed. She was lying so low in the whirlpool only her pale, moon-shaped face showed. "There aren't that many motorcycles on campus. How hard can it be to find the right one?"

"He's going to hurt someone," Deejay added, "I can feel it in my poor, aching bones. I think he's just been toying with people. But sooner or later, that will bore him. Then we're really in for it."

"Oh, he's *not* violent," Echo heard herself saying. "He's just scaring people, that's all."

There was a second of surprised silence before Deejay said, "Echo? Do you know something no one else does?"

"Of course not," she said hastily. She kept her back to the three in the tub. "But he really hasn't hurt anyone, right?"

Another second or two of silence. Then Ruthanne spoke up. "Echo," Ruthanne said slowly, as if she were choosing her words carefully, "now that I think about it, you must know some really weird people. Any of them bikers?"

Startled, Echo looked up from the pile of towels she was folding. "I know some really weird people? What's that supposed to mean?"

Ruthanne failed to look abashed. "Well, when you circulated that silly petition, you must have met lots of people the rest of us don't know."

Meaning, Echo realized, people who weren't "normal." Because if Ruthanne didn't know them, they couldn't possibly be normal. "You're right, Ruthanne," she replied with false brightness. "I *do* know scads of really weird people." She glared pointedly at Ruthanne. "Some *really* weird people."

Ruthanne ignored that. "Any of them own bikes?"

"Almost all of them. I own a bike. You own a bike, Ruthanne. I've seen you riding it, in spite of your arthritis."

Ruthanne sighed, clearly impatient. "I meant a motorcycle, Echo, and you know it. One of those Hailey things. Why do you have to be such a pain all the time?"

"Takes one to know one," Echo muttered under her breath. "Well, maybe I *do* know a biker or two. So what?" The minute the words were out of her mouth, she wanted them back. If Pruitt ever found out she'd said even that much, he'd be furious. He'd cancel her ride, and she was so looking forward to it. It was such a gorgeous spring night.

The girls all pounced on her. "You know a biker?" Deejay sounded astonished. "Who? I've never seen you with anyone on a motorcycle."

Like Deejay paid that much attention to who Echo was spending her free time with. What did Deejay, or any of her friends, know about Echo Glenn's life? When did they ever ask? They had dumped her into the box labelled "Antisocial Activist Slightly on the Weird Side" and left her there. She could be spending her afternoons skywriting obscene messages directly over campus and they wouldn't notice because she wasn't one of *them*.

She wasn't one of them because she wasn't always at the mall, and she didn't join clubs or sororities and she didn't work in campus theater or on the newspaper or at the radio station or sing in the campus Chorale. She didn't have a cute little nickname assigned to her by a bunch of giggling girls, and she didn't have a boyfriend. Hell, she didn't even have parents, at least none to speak of, and all three girls in the whirlpool did.

Not once had they ever asked her about her own family or where she was from or what her major was.

And now Deejay had the gall to pretend she

had ever noticed who Echo was or wasn't with? The only reason Deejay had asked Echo to go to the mall was that even Echo Glenn was better than nobody at all. But Deejay had still ditched her to go to a party.

"All I meant," Echo said forcefully, "was that since today's attack took place on campus, maybe it's someone we know. Someone we *all* know, someone right here at Salem. That's all I meant." Her voice was smooth and slick as glass. "And by the way, Ruthanne," she added as she turned to leave the room, "that happens to be Harley, not Hailey. As in Harley-Davidson. A really gorgeous one, as a matter of fact. And the guy who owns it knows what he's doing. The way he handles that bike is sheer poetry in motion."

She left behind her a shocked silence.

But she took with her an uneasiness. She had said too much. Ruthanne had made her so mad! Great vocabulary or not, the girl was really ditsy.

I shouldn't have let her get to me like that, Echo thought as she threw a load of towels in the washing machine. She doesn't even matter. None of them do. So why do I let them jerk me around?

When she returned to the whirlpool room

after stalling as long as she could, they were gone. The room was empty.

Echo stood in the doorway, wondering how many people they'd already told, "Echo Glenn knows a biker." Unless she was mistaken, the quote would rapidly become, "Echo Glenn, you know, that girl who's always stirring up a fuss on campus, well, she hangs out with bikers. She told us so herself."

Not that she cared what people thought. But if word somehow got back to the administration, possibly even the police, she could be called upon to ask some hard questions. That would *not* be fun.

Whatever. She was going to have her ride, that was all she cared about now.

Echo hurried back to the dorm to dress in jeans, boots, and a sweatshirt. It wasn't a leather jacket, but it would shield her from the wind. Tying her thick, curly hair up in a careless ponytail, she left, so excited her heart was beating erratically. This was going to be *fun!* *If* Pruitt hadn't chickened out. If he was really there.

He was there. He was waiting for her at the brick wall behind the infirmary, helmet on, an extra black helmet in his hand. Even if he'd shouted a hello, which she suspected he hadn't, she'd never have heard him over the roar of the idling engine. Silently, he thrust the helmet at her, and she obediently put it on. Then she climbed on the back of the bike, wrapped her arms around his waist, and, heart pounding, sat back to enjoy the ride.

She understood why, at the end of Campus Drive, he turned the bike left instead of right, toward town. There was nothing in this direction except the state park and acres of uninhabited woods. No one to see them, except an occasional car. This was much safer. She'd have her exciting, windblown drive without the risk of being linked to the Mad Biker.

Echo was sure he was being cautious more for his sake than for hers. It would be stupid of him to venture into town this soon after the chaos he'd created last night at the mall. The Twin Falls police force, small though it was, would be on the look-out for any and all motorcycles, probably stopping them to ask questions even if they weren't speeding.

This direction was safest, for both of them.

The ride was everything Echo had hoped it would be. The wind in her face was exhilarating, the speed thrilling. Even the roar of the engine, making conversation impossible, pleased her. It sounded so incredibly powerful.

She felt freer than she ever had in her life as they raced along the highway, no one watching them but the deep, dark, quiet woods on both sides of the road.

Pruitt attempted no fancy stunts, no bobbing or weaving, no sudden stops. He just drove.

That suited Echo just fine. She didn't need any fancy maneuvers. The ride itself was enough.

What didn't suit her, however, was how short the ride was. It was over much too quickly. Breathless and windblown when Pruitt stopped the bike behind the infirmary and motioned for her to get off, she couldn't help asking, "Just a few more minutes? Couldn't we take a quick ride along the river road behind campus? It's really too early to go in on a Saturday night. Please?"

He seemed to hesitate, then shook his head. "Better not. Time to put this baby to bed. Another time, okay? Let me have the helmet."

Reluctantly, she handed it to him, and the next thing she knew, she was standing there alone while the bike raced off into the distance until it became no more than the faint red dot of its taillight blinking at her out of the darkness.

Echo fought to keep her disappointment

from spoiling the ride. It *had* been wonderful. She should be savoring it instead of hungering for more.

That's your problem, she scolded as she walked slowly back to the dorm. You always want more. You want more from people than they're willing to give, and you want more from life than it's ever going to provide. If you don't change, you are always, always, going to be disappointed.

She was almost to Lester when she heard, coming toward her from the rear, the familiar animal-like roar of the bike's engine. She recognized it immediately, knew it wasn't a car with a bad muffler, or a power mower, or a train on distant tracks. It was the motorcycle, no question.

She whirled, peering into the darkness. Here it came, light on, black-gloved hands on the handlebars. As it reached her and stopped, one snakeskin-booted foot hit the pavement. The helmet she'd worn earlier was thrust at her sheepishly.

Echo laughed with delight. "You changed your mind!" she cried.

He nodded and shrugged carelessly. She had a feeling he might be grinning under the face shield. "Get on!" he shouted over the engine's impatient grumbling.

Echo couldn't obey fast enough. She hopped on behind him, stuffing her hair up underneath the helmet and fastening the strap. She wrapped her arms around his waist again. "Thanks!" she called as he stomped down on the pedal. "Thanks for changing your mind!"

He nodded, and off they went.

But this time, he didn't head for the state park. Nor did he aim for the river road. Instead, she found herself on the back of a motorcycle racing toward town.

"Maybe this isn't such a good idea!" she shouted as they passed Nightingale Hall, a huge, brick, off-campus dorm sitting high on a hill overlooking the highway a short distance from campus. The house had been nicknamed "Nightmare Hall" because of strange occurrences there, including at least one mysterious death. It was a gloomy, dark, dreary old place, and because she knew there had been trouble there, the sight of the house reminded Echo that trouble could also be awaiting them in town. "Maybe we should turn around now and go back!"

Pruitt didn't answer, didn't even shake his head. And he didn't turn the bike around. They kept going in the same direction.

No uniformed police officers were lying in wait for them when they reached Twin Falls.

Late on Saturday night, everyone who was going somewhere had already arrived and the main street, lined with banks and shops and restaurants, was deserted, although the store display windows and the restaurants and the clubs were bright with lights.

Echo breathed a sigh of relief as they stopped at a red light at the bridge in the center of town. If no one saw them, if Pruitt drove on for just a few more minutes and then raced back to campus, it would be all right. Nothing horrible would happen.

The light turned green, and he was off, heading deeper into town, toward the area housing several nightclubs where Salem students went to dance.

Someone might see us, Echo thought. And then what?

"Pruitt!" Echo called over the engine's deafening roar. "I think we should go back! Please, let's go back now!"

He ignored her. Didn't even slow down.

They were approaching a club Echo had heard of, called Johnny's Place, one of the most popular clubs in town. She could see a small group of people gathered on the sidewalk under a green canvas canopy. There were two couples, laughing and talking. It was too early for them to be calling it a night, so Echo decided they must have come outside for a breath of fresh air. She couldn't see them well enough to tell who they were, but she probably didn't know them, anyway. They were "fun" people who went dancing on Saturday nights.

Maybe it was bcause no one had ever asked her to go dancing on a Saturday night or any other night that Echo decided she might wave as they whizzed by the group. Or maybe it was a perverse streak in her that asked her what good it did for her to take a ride with the Mad Biker if no one ever knew about it? They wouldn't know her identity, because the helmet and face shield protected that. But they'd know *someone* was on the back of the bike, and *she'd* know it was her. That would have to be enough.

But she never got the chance to wave.

With a sudden, startling twist of the handlebars, the bike left the road and roared up onto the sidewalk.

It was aiming straight at the group.

Its speed never lessened as it plowed into them.

Echo, all of her senses frozen in shock, saw it all in slow motion, and would see it again, over and over, for a long time to come.

A girl in a bright red dress was tossed through the glass front door of the club, shattering it into a thousand pieces.

A boy in jeans and a blue shirt was thrown up against a tan station wagon parked at the curb, and Echo felt, rather than heard, his bones breaking.

Another boy whom Echo recognized as Liam McCullough sailed straight up into the air on impact, somersaulting into the soft canvas canopy.

It all happened so fast, in less time than it would have taken her to lift her hand and wiggle her fingers in a triumphant, in-your-face kind of wave. Forever after, the scene would blur in her mind like a watercolor left out in the rain.

She came to her senses then and began clawing at the black leather jacket, pounding on Pruitt's shoulders, screaming, screaming at him to stop. "Stop, stop it!" she shrieked. "What are you doing? Oh, God, what are you *doing*?"

The fourth person in the group, a small, slender girl in a bright blue dress and heels, had seen the bike coming and broken into a run. She was still running, high heels impeding her progress, her head repeatedly swivelling over her shoulder to display eyes wide with terror as she checked to see if she had escaped.

She hadn't.

Although Echo continued to claw at the

leather-clad shoulders in front of her, to pound with both fists on the back, to scream and shout at Pruitt to stop, please stop, he bore down upon the girl with a vengeance.

There was nowhere for her to go, nowhere she could hide.

The front wheel of the bike hit her in the back. She wasn't very heavy. The impact lifted her up, out of her heels and sent her, in her stocking feet, up into the air like an oversized, bright blue bird trying to outrace the motorcycle.

The bike slowed, and even in her state of shock, Echo realized why. Pruitt didn't *want* to outrace the girl. He wanted to see her fall back to earth.

Sickened, Echo used her nails to dig viciously into the back of Pruitt's neck, just below the helmet, drawing blood.

He didn't seem to notice.

The girl landed on the sidewalk just ahead of them with an awful, splatting sound.

Voices and running footsteps behind them told Echo that patrons had heard the commotion, left the club, and were pursuing the bike on foot.

Pruitt heard the sounds of pursuit, too.

He gunned the engine and sped away, running over the girl's limp, outstretched legs.

Chapter 5

The shock of the horrifying events took its toll on Echo. She couldn't speak as they raced away from the scene. All of the screaming she had done back there had been in vain, wasted cries that left her throat raw and four people injured, perhaps dead. But even if she could have spoken, that, too, would have been wasted effort. Her brain had been so severely assaulted by what she had seen that no clear thought was possible. Fragments of sentences flew around in her mind like bats in a cave, but she was too stunned to gather them together.

Because her senses were still numbed by the horror of what had happened, the tears she needed to shed, the screams she needed to scream, the fury she needed to give vent to, all remained locked inside of her, churning around until she became physically ill.

By the time they reached Nightmare Hall,

she was reeling with nausea and knew she was about to topple off the bike.

Once again she pounded on the back of Pruitt's jacket.

This time he stopped, coming to a screeching halt at the end of the gravel driveway leading up to the spooky old house.

Echo threw herself off the bike, ripped the helmet off her head, and lurched toward a narrow strip of grass beside a drainage ditch where, on her hands and knees, she lost her sandwich and coffee. Then she collapsed sideways, lying on her back on the grass, breathless and dizzy and weak.

"C'mon, we gotta go," Pruitt called over the loud sputtering of the engine.

"No."

"What?"

Echo covered her eyes with one hand in an effort to shut out the sight of the bike and its rider. "I'm not going anywhere with you. After what you did. . . ."

"Don't you mean what *we* did?"

The question penetrated Echo's consciousness like a wash of acid. We? *We?*

Now she was alert. Yes, there *had* been a we. Whenever more than one person was involved in something, you had a "we," wasn't that right? And Echo Glenn, all by herself, had turned this nightmare into a "we" situation, as in a "couple," as in "he and I," as in "us." There were *two* people on that bike when it smashed into those people, and I was one of the two, she thought. That thought made her sick again.

Pruitt stayed on the bike. He didn't turn off the engine. She could barely hear his voice. "Don't you think you're overreacting just a little?" he said. "If you're worried about getting caught, don't. Nobody but me knows who you are. And I'm not telling. And, of course, you won't be telling about me, either."

Oh, God. Echo rolled over and hid her face in her hands. She couldn't think clearly. But this much her stunned, sick mind grasped: he would use that against her. He *would*.

"Go away," she muttered from behind her hands. "Just go away and leave me alone. You're sick, you're crazy! You have to be to do something so awful. Get away from me!" She struggled upright just long enough to toss the helmet at him, then she collapsed again onto the grass.

He laughed as he caught the helmet. The sound was laden with satisfaction. "I'll go. But don't forget, I was not alone out there tonight. Later."

The bike roared away, and Echo thought, Forget? Forget? How could I ever forget?

She lay on the grass until her legs felt as if they might be willing to hold her upright, then got up slowly. She still felt weak and sick, but she was afraid that someone who lived at Nightmare Hall would come home from a Saturday night date, find her there and ask difficult questions. That fear moved her feet along the berm of the highway toward campus.

As she walked, she couldn't help imagining the scene in town: the bodies strewn everywhere, the shocked patrons of Johnny's Place standing around, watching in horror as ambulances arrived and the victims were loaded into them. Were they all still alive? How could the girl who had tried to outrace the bike possibly still have a breath left in her?

I should have stayed there, Echo told herself in misery as she plodded along the dark road toward campus. *I should have jumped off the bike somehow and stayed to help.*

But Pruitt hadn't slowed down long enough. Maybe he'd somehow sensed that doing so would have given her the opportunity to desert him. And he didn't want that, did he?

He wasn't going to leave her alone now. She was as sure of that as she was that her arms and legs were trembling violently. She fought to steady them. If anyone came along now and saw her stumbling along the highway, they might stop to help her. What possible explanation could she give for being out here alone late on a Saturday night?

Instead of going straight to the dorm and hiding in her bed, which was what she wanted to do more than anything, she headed for the infirmary. The victims had probably been taken to the hospital in town, but on the off chance that the less seriously injured (if there were any) might have been brought to campus, she turned her steps in that direction.

She knew even before she went inside that a patient from Twin Falls had arrived, because there was a Twin Falls EMS truck parked sideways in front of the low, brick building. Had to be a student, or it wouldn't have been brought to campus.

The patient being treated in one of the emergency cubicles, she was told by the student volunteer manning the reception desk, was "that tall, cute guy with the name everyone mispronounces. You know . . . everyone says Lie-am, but it's really Lee-am. Liam McCullough." A tall, heavyset brunette, she leaned across the desk and almost whispered, "There was another biker attack in town tonight. A really bad one this time. He hit *a whole bunch of people*!" She said this with such awe, and her eyes were so round with fascination that Echo felt sick again.

"Liam was one of the people who got hit," the girl, whose plastic black and white name tag read "ANNETTE " said, her tone conversational now. "I think he's got a broken wrist. He was holding his left arm funny. And he had a big lump on his forehead, so maybe he's got a concussion, too."

"What about the others?" Echo had to ask.

"They're at the hospital." Annette's expression sobered. "I heard someone say that Lily D'Agostino might not live." Her eyes widened again. "He hit her, and then he ran right over her, can you believe that? I mean, isn't it just too horrible?"

Yes, Echo thought, clutching the edge of the desk, it is just too horrible. But . . . the girl, the bluebird in flight, hadn't died. Yet. She was still alive. Barely, maybe, but alive.

Echo turned to leave. There wasn't anything she could do here. Might as well go back to the dorm and crawl into bed. If she was really, really lucky, she might even sleep a little.

The first thing she did in her room was switch on the radio. She had missed the initial story, but because the victims were students, the campus radio station would present updates every fifteen minutes.

While she waited, she took off her shoes and socks and flopped down on the bed. There was a huge, hollow space inside of her that she knew would fill up with pain and terror and regret and guilt the very second that shock left her. If it ever did.

Although the window was open and the night was very warm, she pulled the rose and blue afghan her grandmother had knit for her up to her chin, hoping it would erase the dreadful iciness deep inside of her, and knowing that it wouldn't. No artificial warmth, no matter how heavy, could reach that frozen place.

The music ended, and the announcer's deep, authoritative voice filled the room.

Echo listened to it in misery.

"The latest in a series of unexplained motorcycle attacks on the populace of Twin Falls and the surrounding area has taken its toll this evening. Three students from Salem University have been admitted to the community hospital, and a fourth was taken to the campus infirmary following a particularly vicious attack on Tenth Street in front of the popular nightspot, Johnny's Place."

Echo huddled deeper into the folds of her afghan, one clenched fist pressing against her mouth.

"Two of the students at the hospital are listed

in fair condition, while a third, whose name has not been released pending notification of relatives, is in the intensive care unit, in critical condition."

Critical condition. Echo knew what that meant. It meant that Lily D'Agostino might not make it, after all. She could die at any moment.

Why was that such a shock? Why was she trembling violently again? How could she have expected anything else after seeing, with her own eyes, that poor girl struck in the back by the bike, tossed up into the air and flung back down to the sidewalk, only to be run over by the wheels of the bike?

It was a miracle that Lily D'Agostino wasn't already dead.

"Police in Twin Falls have released a statement reading, in part, that a concentrated effort to find the perpetrators of this vicious crime has begun, and that anyone having any information about the motorcycle or the bikers in question should contact the police station immediately."

Use of the plural was not lost on Echo. "Perpetrators," he had said. "Bikers in question."

They were, now, looking for two people.

She turned off the radio and buried her face in her pillow.

She was one of those people.

Still, the police didn't know that. Or they'd be knocking on her door right now.

No one in that group could possibly have recognized her. She'd been wearing jeans and a sweatshirt. Nothing distinctive there. Everyone wore that kind of clothing on campus. And she'd had the helmet on, her hair tucked up underneath it. The face shield had hidden her features.

Besides, none of the four knew her that well. The only person in that group she'd ever talked to, up close, was Liam McCullough, and he'd been so angry at her the day she'd run into him on the river path, he probably hadn't been paying all that much attention to what she looked like. He couldn't possibly have recognized her tonight.

Echo rolled over on her side, facing the wall. Unlike Trixie, who had plastered every square inch of the wall beside her bed with high school photos, posters of movie stars and rock groups and magazine articles on how to accentuate your best features or how to do your makeup so it looked "natural," the wall beside Echo's bed was bare. She could stare at it and be distracted by nothing. She had, in the past, found that soothing.

But not tonight, not now, because the bare

white wall was the perfect screen for images of the destruction wrought on Tenth Street in Twin Falls earlier that night. Once, twice, three times, the event played itself out in front of Echo's eyes, as if she were watching a movie. She saw every detail, far more clearly than she had when it actually happened. And she heard sounds that hadn't registered then, like teeth clicking violently together when the boy was thrown up against the station wagon, and the scream of the girl who had been tossed through the glass door of Johnny's Place.

But she's still alive, Echo told herself, she *is*, the radio said so. Doesn't that mean that it wasn't as bad as it looked?

It couldn't have been. Couldn't have been as bad as it looked.

Unable to bear the sight replaying itself on her wall, Echo threw herself over on her stomach.

But the sights were in her mind, not on the wall itself, and, like a defective VCR stuck on "replay," the scene played itself over and over again, all through the long, long night, adding new and more gruesome details each time.

Echo never slept at all.

Chapter 6

Echo crawled out of bed on Sunday morning after the longest night of her life with a headache and swollen eyes. She had cried, after all, when the images replaying themselves in her mind had finally overwhelmed her. The tears spilling out of her felt strange and unsettling, as if she were being drained of a part of herself. Frightened by that feeling, she had stopped and wiped her eyes. But every now and then during the night, the tears had come again.

It was the first time she had really cried since her mother left her at her grandparents' house, saying, "You be a good girl now. Don't give Nana and Papa any trouble."

But I did, Echo thought with sudden clarity. I gave them lots of trouble, practically every minute. I punished them for not being my parents, and it wasn't even their fault.

Still, that trouble she'd given her grandparents: staying out too late, sleeping in on week-ends when her grandmother could have used some help with the housework or errands, ignoring her homework until teachers called the house to complain, mouthing off for very little reason, dating the "wrong" boys, not because she liked them especially, but because she knew perfectly well everyone would consider them the "wrong" boys . . . all of that was peanuts compared to the trouble she was in now. She was in this one up to her neck.

Now she knew how people felt when they were drowning.

And there wasn't anyone to throw her a life preserver, was there?

Your choice, Echo, a stern voice reminded her. *You* were the one who didn't want any close friends.

True. And she didn't want any now, either, because anyone who was really close to her would be able to see in her eyes that she'd been on Tenth Street last night on the back of a murderous motorcycle.

I will get out of this one myself, she vowed, throwing the afghan aside and hauling herself out of bed. Just like I always do. I *will*!

But she had no idea how.

There was only one person she could talk to about this. Pruitt. Not because he was a friend,

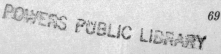

oh, God, he was no friend of hers, but because, like it or not, he had shared the horrible experience. The last person in the world she wanted to see on this warm, sunny morning was Aaron Pruitt. But there wasn't anyone else.

Echo had heard the expression, "Politics makes strange bedfellows." She wasn't exactly sure what that meant. Something about all the wheeling and dealing that went on in politics making it necessary for people who didn't really have anything in common to hang out together. It occurred to her now that the same could be said for crime. Pruitt was not someone she would ever have been interested in if not for the bike, and if it hadn't been for her interest in the bike, she wouldn't have been on Tenth Street last night in the first place. Now here she was, stuck in this weird, uneasy alliance with someone she wouldn't normally give the time of day to, someone she really hated for what he'd done.

How could she make Pruitt disappear from her life? More important, how could she make last night disappear? Erase it from her life, and from the lives of the injured four?

She couldn't.

Feeling incredibly heavy, as if her body were suddenly encased in a coat of metal, Echo dressed in the jeans she found on the floor and a clean blue T-shirt. She ran her fingers, but not a brush or comb, through her hair as she left the room. What difference did it make how she looked?

She found Pruitt sitting on the low stone wall around the fountain on the Commons. He was reading, his head bent over a textbook. The wide, grassy area between the tall, stone buildings was crowded with sun worshippers, Frisbee players, and joggers. At first, it struck Echo as odd that no one looked particularly upset by what had happened the night before. And then she realized that any close friends of the four victims wouldn't be out here goofing off. They'd be at the hospital or the infirmary, visiting the injured.

She really didn't want to be seen talking to Pruitt. Not a good idea.

"Meet me behind the infirmary wall," she said in a low voice as she passed him without stopping. "Now." Then she went on to the wall herself. As she passed the infirmary, she breathed a quick sigh of relief that she didn't have to work that day. Liam McCullough was probably still a patient there. Being around him would make her more of a basket case than she already was, if that was possible. Maybe he'd remember that she'd already run into him once on a bike. That might make it easier for him to place her on that motorcycle last night.

She couldn't take that chance.

Pruitt came around the corner of the wall shortly after she did.

"What's up?" he said lazily, leaning against the brick.

She regarded him with cold eyes. "What's *up*? How can you even ask that? Four people are in hospital beds right now, thanks to you. One of them might die."

"We're all going to die, Echo. Sooner or later." His voice was emotionless. "I mean, you were there, right? You saw the whole thing. Did she look to you like she was going to die?"

"You *ran* right over her!"

Pruitt lifted his shoulders nonchalantly. "The guy on the radio last night said she 'failed to get out of the way of the bike.' Sounded to me like he thought it was *her* fault."

Echo's mouth dropped open. "You were on the *sidewalk*! You went after those people on purpose. They never had a chance. How can you blame *them*?"

He turned his back on her, began etching invisible letters on the brick with an index finger. "So," he said lazily, "you up for another ride? Great day for it!"

Echo stared at his back. "You've got to be

kidding! You don't even feel the least bit guilty about what you did last night, do you?"

He turned to face her. "When I drove into that crowd at the mall, you said it wasn't my fault they fell all over themselves trying to get out of the way. Changed your mind? Don't find motorcycles so fascinating anymore, Echo?"

"Those people last night didn't get hurt trying to get out of your way. You went straight for them! They never had a chance. And only someone who is really twisted wouldn't feel guilty about doing what you did."

He smiled thinly. "Meaning me, I guess. Sick and twisted, that's me."

Echo made a sound of contempt. "If the boot fits . . ."

The smile, which struck her as incredibly cold and humorless, stretched into a grin. "That's cute. Of course, you're not planning on going to the police about the boot fitting Aaron Pruitt's foot." It was a statement, not a question.

She hadn't decided yet. She couldn't think clearly enough to formulate a way out of this mess. Still, she said with false bravado, "I'm not? Why not?" She needed to know what he was thinking. She couldn't tell just by looking at him, the way you could with some people. Nothing showed in his thin, pale face.

He sat down on the grass in front of the wall, linking his arms around his bended knees. "Look, let's face facts here. You're not stupid, any more than I am. You already *knew* about the other bike incidents. So you had to know coming to me, practically begging me for a ride, climbing on that bike, could lead to trouble. And you got on, anyway. You're no innocent victim here, Echo. You took part in a crime, and in the eyes of the law, you're as guilty as I am. You should know that."

"I *didn't* take part!" she shouted, and then, frightened that someone passing by might have heard her, quickly lowered her voice. "I didn't take part. I had no idea you were going to do something so awful. The other times, all you did was scare people. Even when I saw what you were doing, there was no way I could have jumped off that bike. I'd have been hurt, too, maybe even killed."

Although the sight of him repelled her, she couldn't take her eyes off his face. He was sitting there on the grass, looking up at her so innocently, and the worst part, the very worst part, was that she knew he was right. She *had* asked him for the ride when she already knew he'd been flirting with trouble. Wasn't that one of the things that had intrigued her about the bike episodes? Some guy in black leather and a helmet, driving a gorgeous, powerful bike so close to the edge without actually going over it?

She should have figured that if he gave her the ride she'd asked for, she just might be with him when he did go over that edge.

What kind of a lawyer was she going to make if she couldn't judge people and situations any better than that?

Maybe now, she would never *be* a lawyer. Maybe she had no future. "It wasn't my fault," she said shakily. "You were the one who was driving."

He laughed with scorn. "Get real, Echo. Who's going to believe that was me on that bike? Aaron Pruitt? No one on this campus has ever seen me near a motorcycle. Their eyes would fall out of their head if they *did* see it."

He's right, Echo thought, no one would believe that Aaron Pruitt was the Mad Biker.

"Now you, on the other hand," he said, his hands toying with a blade of grass, "would make an excellent suspect, it seems to me. So go ahead and tell the police, if you want. See how much good it'll do you. But my guess is, if you walk into the police station in town, you'll be hanging yourself, not me."

"I don't even *own* a motorcycle."

"How would you ever prove that? The cops

would just think you'd ditched the bike somewhere. So, without any proof to link *me* to last
night, you'd go down alone."

Echo mulled his words over in her mind.
What scared her the most about them was that
they made sense. Who would believe that bor-
ing, neatnik Aaron Pruitt would have the guts
or the imagination to be the Mad Biker? But
almost anyone who knew her or knew *of* her
would readily believe that Echo Glenn had been
riding on the back of that bike. Even if she
gave the police Pruitt's name, they'd never find
any proof against him. She might very well go
down alone, just as he said.

Echo fell into a miserable silence.

While she was thinking, Pruitt began enum-
erating aloud her many offenses: first circulating the infamous petition, then her very vocal
denouncing of the administration from the campus library steps for not cooperating. She had
almost started a riot, and the Twin Falls police
had been called to campus. Then he related, in
graphic detail, the afternoon in January when
Echo had jumped up on a table in Lester's caf-
eteria to decry what she had called "the slop
we're being fed in this dungeon." He followed
up with the story about her running into Liam
McCullough on her bike.

"How do you know all that?" Echo demanded.

"I checked around. You also have no close friends and would never win the Miss Congeniality award in any beauty pageant. Although," he added, "you might win for looks, I guess. There are some stunning bones in that pretty face."

Echo stiffened. "Maybe you're right," she said coldly. "Maybe no one would believe that you had anything to do with the bike attacks. But I still think all I'd have to do is raise suspicion and you wouldn't dare go near that bike again. Wouldn't that spoil all your fun?"

In a split second, he was on his feet and at her side. His left hand came up and gripped her elbow with iron fingers. "You make as much trouble for me as you have for the administration of this university and you will be very, very sorry. Let me make this *very* clear. Trouble for me could be very hazardous to those good looks I just mentioned, Echo. After last night, you know what being hit by a Harley at high speed can do. Just think what it could do to those gorgeous cheekbones of yours."

Too stunned to speak, Echo remained silent.

Pruitt let go of her elbow and backed away. His face was flushed, and Echo noticed that his hands were shaking. But when he spoke again, his voice was calm. "You can't hurt me, Echo. But I could finish *you* off, just like that," snapping his fingers. He sat back down again. "With you dead, I could pin that whole incident last night on *you*. But . . ." he grinned at her, "if I did that right now, I wouldn't be able to have any more fun, would I? That would mean the end of my days as a wild biker. So don't worry. I'll have to let you live, for now. And maybe for as long as you behave yourself." He studied her carefully, then smiled a long, slow smile. "Now that I think about it," his words coming slowly, thoughtfully, "I wouldn't mind being seen at the campus movie tonight with someone who looks like you. Might get me some attention for a change."

A black cloud descended over Echo. The sun was still shining above her, but she felt chilled to the bone. "I'm not going anywhere with you."

"Oh, I think you are. Wherever I say, actually. Now that you know how hazardous to your health I can be, I don't think you're going to cross me, are you, Echo? That would be foolish." He was looking very pleased with himself, his pale eyes behind the wire-rimmed glasses taking on a dreamy quality. "Yes, I think that being seen with you will really up my image. Let's see . . . a movie tonight, maybe the dance at the rec center next Friday night, then, who knows? This could develop into a really productive relationship for both of us, Echo. Pick me up at the frat house at seven. Be on time."

And with a casual wave of his hand, he walked away.

He walked jauntily, as if he didn't have a care in the world.

Well, why not? she thought bitterly. Isn't he practically getting away with murder? If Lily dies, it *will* be murder. And now I'm next on the list.

She couldn't go to that movie with him.

She sat down on a stone garden bench surrounding a bed of bright red flowers. What choice did she have? If she didn't go, he'd come after her on that bike, maybe not tonight, maybe not even tomorrow night, but sometime soon. She knew it. She could feel it. That look on his face when she'd threatened to cast suspicion on him would stay in her mind forever. He had meant that look.

She couldn't go to the police. She had absolutely *no* proof that Pruitt had been driving that motorcycle. Even if she could convince the cops to talk to Pruitt, he'd know perfectly well who had sent them and she'd be finished.

Where was she going to get proof that Aaron Pruitt wasn't who everyone thought he was?

This was a scary, scary mess she'd got herself into. Even if she didn't end up in prison, even if she could somehow prove that the real villain was Pruitt and convince the authorities that she hadn't known what he was going to do at Johnny's Place, she'd be expelled for having any part in the tragic, horrible incident.

And then what would she do? Where would she go? Back to her grandparents'? They had their own problems, and they wouldn't welcome her when they found out she'd been kicked out of school.

She had to stay at Salem. She *had* to!

Get a grip, Echo, she warned silently. Okay, so she couldn't go to the authorities until she had some proof. She would have to *find* proof.

How?

Echo stood up. If she spent some time with Pruitt, revolting as the thought was, she just might learn something. Like . . . like where he might have hidden that bike. If she had the bike, she could go to the police with it. He'd said it wasn't registered in his name, but didn't the police have ways of finding out things even when you didn't want them to? Her criminology class first semester had had a lot to do with forensic science. If there were fingerprints anywhere on that bike, if there was a single hair from Pruitt's head in the helmet hanging from the handlebars, the police could connect him to it.

That wouldn't let her off the hook. She'd still be an accessory. But if she came forward with the identity of the biker, wouldn't that improve her chances of staying at Salem? Prove that she was, after all, a good citizen who cared about justice?

Without the bike, she had no chance at all.

With the bike, she had a tiny chance.

And the only chance she had of finding the bike was hanging around Pruitt.

Echo left the bench and began walking slowly back to Lester. There was a problem. Being seen on campus with Pruitt and attending a movie in his company was a terrible idea. It linked her with him. It would make it look like they were friends. Later, when she turned in the bike, if she found it, everyone would assume they'd planned last night's attack together.

But if she didn't go to the movie, he would come after her. She could feel it in her bones . . . the same bones he had threatened to crush with the bike.

The prospect of Pruitt aiming that deadly machine at her was a lot scarier than being linked romantically with him.

She would go to the movie. But she wouldn't look happy about it. Later, when the question of their "association" came up, people might remember that she had looked like she was miserable. Maybe that would help.

Remembering Pruitt's newly arrogant walk, Echo thought, What choice do I have?

There didn't seem to be one.

Chapter 7

There were only two people in the shiny red Miata parked at the edge of an overlook above campus. They were arguing. The driver, a heavyset, blond male in jeans and a Salem T-shirt, repeatedly shouted and waved his arms angrily toward the ant-like people playing tennis or tossing a Frisbee or jogging far below the outcropping on which the car rested.

"Look at them down there," the boy, whose name was Polk Malone, accused vehemently. "They're having *fun*! And we're sitting up here twiddling our thumbs because you didn't feel like doing anything. You never want to do anything fun!" The car windows were rolled down, and the sound of his shout carried into the late afternoon silence, startling the wildlife living in the woods on the hilltop.

The girl, Nancy Becker, small and also blonde, was in tears. But they were angry tears. "When we played tennis," she shouted back, "you blamed me because we lost to Ian and Jess. When we played golf, you said I lost too many balls. At Johnny's Place the other night, you flirted with Ruthanne all night. I never should have dumped Aaron for *you*! He's a lot nicer than you are."

"Aaron Pruitt is a geek! You should thank me for saving you from him. Every time I pass him on the Commons, he looks at me like he'd like to string me up. Like that makes me shake in my shoes."

The bump, when it came, might have gone unnoticed in the heat of their argument if Polk hadn't been far more concerned about his shiny red Miata than he was about making up with Nancy. There were plenty of other girls on campus, but what were his chances of getting another car from his dad if something happened to this one?

"Hey!" he shouted indignantly when the bump came. "What was that?"

Nancy swiped at her angry tears. "What? What was what?"

Polk's eyes flew to the rearview mirror. "Someone hit us from behind."

"I didn't feel anything."

Bump! It came again, a little harder, jostling the car slightly.

"Oh. I felt that one," Nancy said, her head swivelling to glance backward. "There's someone back there, Polk."

Polk's expression was grim. "It's a motorcycle."

Nancy drew in her breath sharply. "Polk! A motorcycle?" Her face visibly paled. "It's not that crazy biker, is it?"

Polk didn't ask who she meant. "Nah. That guy wears black leather, I heard. This jerk behind us just has a sweatshirt on. And a helmet. Can't see his face, but it's just some jerk, fooling around."

"Are you sure?"

"I'm sure." Polk was about to add, "Stay in the car. I'll handle this," when another, much more forceful push came from behind, and the Miata slid forward half an inch or so.

Nancy gasped and grabbed the dashboard. Her eyes darted fearfully to the vast, empty void lying straight ahead of them at the edge of the cliff. That void led to a sheer drop straight down . . . "Polk! The car moved! Do something!"

"He doesn't even have his engine on," Polk commented in wonder, his own eyes still fastened to the rearview mirror. "That's why we didn't hear him coming. What's he up to? He can't be serious about it or he'd have his engine on, wouldn't he?"

"How should I know?" Nancy snapped, still clutching the dashboard. "I've never been on one of those things in my life. But it looks awfully big and heavy to me, and this car is small. Didn't I ask you not to park so close to the edge? You never listen to me!"

"What the *hell* is he doing?" Polk murmured, his own face losing some of its color. He moved then to jump out of the car and confront the biker. But a sudden, forceful blow from behind snapped Polk's head forward and slammed it into the steering wheel. He let out a startled grunt. A second later, his eyes snapped shut. His mouth fell open and his head rolled to one side and then lay still.

Nancy, sitting sideways on the front seat, screamed his name. When he didn't answer, her terrified eyes flew to the back window.

The biker was still out there. She could see his helmeted head.

Instinct told her to flee the car. But she was afraid to. *He* was out there. Sweatshirt or not, she knew it was him. He had almost killed Lily D'Agostino last night. He would kill her, too, if she got out of the car. And she couldn't abandon Polk, anyway.

With shaking fingers, Nancy fumbled behind her for her seat belt, which she had removed when they parked. She called Polk's name over and over again as she tried, failed, tried again and finally succeeded in fastening the belt. Then she reached across, still urging Polk to "Wake up, wake up!" to gently lift his head and fasten his own belt around his chest and shoulders.

She was just sliding the clasp into place when the motorcycle's engine roared to life behind the car.

Nancy sat up very straight. Her head turned slowly toward the back of the car, her eyes wide with dread. "No," she whispered, "no . . ."

Then, for just one tiny little second, hope sprang to life as she watched the bike move away from the car, backing across the road until it reached the edge of the woods on the other side.

He's going to turn around, she thought, her eyes never leaving the motorcycle. Her body was shaking so violently with fear, her knees were banging against each other. She couldn't stop trembling. Her breath came in tiny little gasps. "Polk," she whispered to the boy lying unconscious behind her, "it's going to be okay. He's going to turn around now and drive back down the highway and then you'll wake up and thank me for putting your seatbelt on and you won't be mad at me anymore. We'll drive straight back to campus and I promise I'll play tennis or golf or go dancing or any fun thing that you want." She was sobbing quietly now, as she watched the biker with agonizing anxiety. Her voice rose until she was speaking almost as loudly as Polk had during their argument. "And nothing bad is going to happen because he's going to turn around and go away, he is, I can tell, but if you'd just wake up, Polk, why don't you wake *up*, then I wouldn't have to wait all by myself to see what he's going to do."

The biker did not turn around and drive back down the highway. He just sat there, staring at the car, his engine idling and snoring noisily and spewing out black smoke. He stared at the car for a long time, two, three, four minutes, while the terrified girl in the car kept her eyes on him, never taking them off him for a second.

She was praying aloud now, because he hadn't left, and so she was praying for him to leave, "Please, please, let him leave, please, I want to get out but I'm scared, I'm so scared if I get out he'll run me down, break my legs like he did Lily's, and I can't leave Polk, anyway, please, please, just make him go away and I promise I'll never ask for anything else again as long as I live."

She was still praying aloud when the biker gunned his engine, and flew across the highway, slamming into the back of the Miata at full speed.

Nancy screamed. She swivelled on the seat and threw herself on top of Polk. Maybe she hoped to protect him. Or maybe she was willing him to wake up and protect her.

The car lurched forward and sailed off the edge of the cliff as if it had suddenly sprouted wings. But without power, it only hung in the air for a second or two before plummeting down, down, straight down.

The haunting wail of Nancy Becker's voice giving up all hope wrapped itself around the car during the long descent.

When the bright red machine landed in a deep ravine across the highway from campus, it bounced several times like a red rubber ball, then exploded in a giant red and yellow fireball.

The roaring flames consuming Polk's beloved red Miata were no threat to Nancy Becker and Polk Malone, though. Because they were both already dead, killed instantly in the violent impact.

The biker sat at the very edge of the overlook and watched as, far below him, flames gobbled up the Miata and its occupants.

Then he sped away into the gray-blue dusk, leaving a trail of black smoke in his wake.

Chapter 8

"You're going out with who?" Trixie asked in disbelief.

"Whom," a nervous Echo corrected automatically. She wrestled her hair up into a haphazard topknot. "I keep forgetting you're not an English major."

"No. Psych. And I wish I'd learned enough already to figure out why on earth you'd be going out with someone like Aaron Pruitt. Deejay and Marilyn couldn't believe it, either, and Ruthanne almost had a stroke. He's a friend of theirs, I guess, but he's so . . . so . . ."

"So *not* gorgeous and *not* charming and *not* athletic?" Echo suggested, an edge to her voice. "Well, that's okay, Trixie, because as you and I both know, *I'm* not exactly Miss Popularity, myself." Of course that didn't make her a maniac, like Pruitt.

Trixie had the decency to flush. "I . . . I didn't mean . . ."

"Whatever." Echo dug into her scalp with the edge of a bobby pin and winced. But it was her anger she felt the most. Until now, she had planned to make it clear to everyone who saw her at the rec center that night that she wasn't with Pruitt willingly. She hadn't been sure exactly how to do that, except by looking as if she were having a lousy time, which she was sure wouldn't be a problem. But now, she felt a sudden, fierce need to defy Trixie. It would be different if Trixie knew what Pruitt had done. Then she'd have reason to hate and fear him. But Trixie *didn't* know that. Only Echo did.

The trouble was, she had no idea what to do with that knowledge.

"Anyway, I finally found out how Pruitt got into a fraternity," Trixie said. "I always wondered. He doesn't seem like the type. But Dee-jay told me his father is loaded. Pruitt and Banner Investments?"

"Never heard of them."

Trixie's expression said, "Well, no, you wouldn't have, would you?"

"Pruitt, Senior, is a Salem alumnus. And a Sigma Chi. That's how Pruitt, Junior, got into Sigma Chi."

"Thank you for sharing that, Trixie. See ya!" And Echo was out the door.

Mistake, she told herself angrily as she entered the elevator. Big, big mistake. I should have said she was right about Pruitt and I was only going out with him as an experiment, to see what makes a geek like that tick. Trixie will remember I got defensive. It'll be the first thing she thinks of if I find that motorcycle and turn Pruitt in to the cops. I can just hear her telling everyone, "Well, you know, there *were* two people on that bike in front of Johnny's Place and one of them could have been a girl, and Echo *was* dating Pruitt, and did she ever get ticked when I made a silly little crack about her going out with him. She got *very* defensive." Trixie would toss her head in that way she had and add, "Of course, since I've lived with her since the very beginning of the year, I know her better than anyone on campus and I can tell you that becoming a wild biker is *just* the sort of thing that would appeal to Echo Glenn!"

When am I going to learn to keep my mouth shut? Echo asked the mirror in the lobby when she passed it.

The minute she stepped outside, she heard sirens. More than one. Off-campus, but close enough that the sound was unmistakable.

Echo stopped, looked around. She smelled smoke. And . . . gasoline.

Off to her left, across the road from campus and into the woods, a huge black cloud of smoke rose up from the trees. A fire? There had been a burning ban on for most of the spring because of dry conditions, but recent rains had ended that edict.

A boy jogging past her slowed and commented, "Looks like that smoke's coming from the ravine. Accident, maybe. That dirt road that runs alongside the ravine is treacherous."

Echo didn't know the woods on that side of the road that well, so she didn't answer, and he went on his way.

Accident? How awful. She hoped no one had been hurt. People said that ravine was very deep and rocky. It wouldn't be a pleasant place to land if your car skidded off the road.

Since there didn't seem to be anything she could do about whatever had happened, she kept going.

Aaron Pruitt's room at the frat house was as neat as Echo would have expected. A dime would have bounced easily on his perfectly made bed. There were no clothes on the floor, only thick, pale gray carpeting. There were no books and notebooks piled high on every flat surface, as there were in Echo's room and in almost every other dorm room she'd ever visited. Two heavy wooden bookcases lined one wall. Echo wouldn't have been surprised to find the books arranged alphabetically. They weren't, but they were orderly.

Her eyes casually skimmed the titles. "Are all those books yours?"

Pruitt's hair was even neater than usual. He shook his head, and not one strand moved. "No. They were already here. Belong to the frat house. Except for a couple dozen I brought with me and the ones I've borrowed from the library." He gestured toward a neat stack on a middle shelf. "Due Wednesday. Hope I don't forget."

"You won't," Echo said flatly, glancing at those titles, too. One held her interest longer than the others. "You're not the type." And then realized how silly that was. The guy was practically a murderer. Why would he have any qualms about returning books late? She kept forgetting that he wasn't the Pruitt she and everyone else had thought he was.

You had darned well better keep that in mind, she warned. Forgetting it could be . . . Echo shivered. She didn't want to think about it.

The evening was every bit as miserable as she had thought it would be. The worst moment was when she walked with Pruitt into the rec center, which was far too crowded to suit Echo, and all heads turned in their direction. He seemed to delight in the attention. Shoulders back, a smug grin on his thin face, he imprisoned Echo's hand in his and casually made his way to the front of the room, where he insisted they take seats in the second row.

"We didn't have to sit so far up front," Echo, rigid with embarrassment, whispered as they sat down. "You just *love* all this attention, don't you?"

"Yes!" he whispered back. "You might as well learn to love it, too. I think we're going to become an item."

Not if I can help it, Echo thought grimly. She could hardly wait for the movie to end. She had to find that motorcycle and disable it somehow, then take the police to wherever Pruitt had hidden it. And now, thanks to the library books in Pruitt's room, she knew where to begin searching. He had to have taken those books out for a reason. Maybe he was just doing a report and needed them for research. But maybe not. It was worth a shot.

But she certainly couldn't begin hunting while Pruitt had a death grip on her hand.

His hand was so cold, almost icy. Echo decided that was because Pruitt had no heart and without a heart, no warm, pulsating blood pumped through his veins. Ice water, she thought, tugging against his hand in vain, that's ice water in there.

The movie and the evening dragged on interminably. Once, Echo glanced over her shoulder in the darkened rec center and saw in the reflected light from the screen, Liam McCullough, sitting one row behind her and off to her right. He was out of the infirmary already. Couldn't have been too badly injured, after all. Now if only Lily D'Agostino got that lucky.

Liam saw her staring at him and nodded curtly.

Echo's head whipped around to the front. She didn't want him wondering why she was staring at him. He might start thinking, even asking questions. That would not be good.

Pruitt insisted on taking her to Vinnie's pizza restaurant after the movie. Echo tried to plead fatigue, but he dismissed her objections by reminding her that she had little choice. "I'm not ready to call it a night," he told her coldly, "and since you're with me, you're not ready to call it a night, either."

Visions of Lily D'Agostino trying to outrun the bike danced before Echo's eyes.

She went to Vinnie's with him.

In the restaurant, they sat with a group of

Pruitt's frat brothers and their dates, including Deejay, Ruthanne, and Marilyn. No one at the table seemed to pay that much attention when Pruitt drew up two chairs and pushed them into the center of the group. The girls from the whirlpool room told Echo "hi" and then returned to their conversation. Only Ruthanne shot Echo an inquiring look, which Echo ignored.

While they waited for their pizza, Echo told herself it was only her imagination making her think that Liam McCullough, sitting at a table opposite theirs, was staring at her. He didn't know anything, couldn't know anything. So why would he be staring at her?

"Quit looking over there," Pruitt hissed in her ear. He squeezed her hand painfully. Echo winced. "It's rude to stare at other guys when you have a date." He glared in Liam's direction. "I see he's recovered. Too bad."

"I suppose you were hoping he'd died," Echo whispered. "He looks very much alive to me."

"You wouldn't want me to think he was competition, would you?" he murmured as their pizza arrived and the clamor for the best slices drowned out his words. "I have my ways of dealing with competition, Echo. You wouldn't want to see McCullough back in the infirmary, would you? Or worse?"

Echo felt her knees begin to tremble under the table. "Competition?" she said lightly. "Don't be silly. I don't even know the guy. Anyway, he hates me."

"Good. Keep it that way. Now eat up, before it's all gone."

Echo didn't touch the pizza. Her stomach was churning with impatience, and the atmosphere at the table did nothing to stimulate her appetite. Ruthanne kept bringing up the subject of the biker.

And then Marilyn said, "Did you hear about those two kids who went off Lookout Point?"

In the act of reaching for her glass of water, Echo's hand stopped in midair, as if someone had just rapped her knuckles with a ruler. "What two kids?"

Marilyn, satisfaction in her eyes because she was now the center of attention, answered, "Polk Malone and Nancy Becker. That disgusting biker pushed them off a cliff. A jogger running up there saw him racing down the hill a second or two after the crash."

Echo was too stunned to speak. "Oh no," she breathed. She deliberately avoided Pruitt's eyes, but she heard him draw in his breath sharply.

"Nancy?" he said. "Nancy Becker was in Polk Malone's car?"

"Oh, sorry, Pruitt," Deejay said then. "I forgot. You knew her, didn't you?"

He didn't answer.

"When?" Echo said. "When did it happen?"

"Late this afternoon. The car smashed into that ravine beside Rockridge Road. I heard they were both killed instantly. And there isn't anything left of the car but ashes."

Echo felt sick and dizzy. The smoke . . . the sirens . . . that had been a car burning. A car with two people in it. Two *dead* people. And one of them had been someone Pruitt *knew*!

"That guy get the biker's license plate?" Pruitt asked Marilyn. "The guy who saw the biker, I mean."

"How should I know? And," she added grimly, "I heard that if Lily D'Agostino lives, she'll be a quadraplegic. Paralyzed from the neck down." Marilyn shuddered.

"Well, what she did was pretty stupid," Pruitt said crudely. "Guy on the radio said she tried to outrun that bike." He seemed to have recovered quickly from the news of Nancy Becker's horrible death.

Several people at the table shook their heads in disgust.

"Even if Lily isn't paralyzed," Ruthanne said almost absentmindedly, "she'll probably be in pain for the rest of her life. I know what that's like. Sometimes, it'll get so bad, she'll wish she *had* died."

Maybe she'll get her wish, Echo thought dismally.

Turning her attention to Echo, Marilyn asked, "By the way, Echo, did you ever remember if you knew any bikers?" To the others, she said in a confidential voice. "Echo thought maybe she knew some, so *I* thought maybe she's met the Mad Biker, only she doesn't know it. I mean, he certainly wouldn't come right out and admit that's who he is, right?"

Pruitt gripped Echo's hand so cruelly, she thought he was going to break her fingers. I *didn't* tell, she wanted to shout, I didn't! Instead, she said to Marilyn, "We must all know one or two people who ride motorcycles, Marilyn, but, as you just pointed out, unless we actually see them on their bikes, we wouldn't know it, would we?"

In the restroom later, Deejay said, "I think it's good that you're with Pruitt, Echo. I mean, he hasn't dated at all since Nancy Becker broke up with him. They only dated once or twice, but I know he had a thing for her. He told me so. So I'm glad he's not alone tonight."

Deejay bent from the waist to brush her short, dark hair and Echo stared into the mirror. Nancy Becker, the recently deceased Nancy Becker, had given Pruitt the old heave-ho? And now she was dead. And Deejay was afraid he'd be really upset?

I don't *think* so, Echo thought, her hands trembling as she finger-combed her own hair. She didn't want to believe this. Cold-blooded murder? Was Pruitt really *that* sick?

He would know she believed he had pushed that Miata off the cliff. Could she pretend she hadn't guessed? No. She wasn't that good an actress. Had he done it because Nancy had dumped him? Or had he done it to show Echo that he meant business?

Maybe both.

Without saying good-bye to Deejay, Echo roused herself enough to leave the restroom, make her excuses, and insisted that she and Pruitt leave the restaurant. She really didn't care if anyone thought that was weird. She just wanted to get out of there.

But once she was outside, her skin went clammy at the thought of walking back to campus alone with him. She wouldn't mention Polk and Nancy, she wouldn't! She would just pretend it hadn't happened.

"Did you do it?" she said, the words spilling out of her mouth of their own volition. "Did you push that car off the cliff?"

He grabbed her hand and wouldn't let go. "What do you think? You know she dumped me, don't you? I can tell. Someone told you. Deejay, probably, when you were in the bathroom. Do you really think I'd let someone do that to me and get away with it?"

He said this as calmly, as unemotionally as he might have said, "Vinnie's has the best pizza in town."

"I don't know," she answered stiffly. "I don't know you well enough to guess what you would or wouldn't do." But she did. That was the problem. She *did*.

"Well, you will. You will." He glanced down at her as they crossed the highway. "I mean, you wouldn't want to end up in a ravine, would you?"

If they talked about Polk and Nancy another second, Echo was going to scream. Instead, she said boldly, "That was a really rotten thing to say about Lily. Aren't you afraid people will guess how hardhearted you really are?"

He shrugged. "It's true, isn't it? She tried to outrun the bike and didn't make it. What's so bad about saying that?"

Echo was so sure she could never make him understand, she didn't even try. All she wanted to do now was get rid of him and begin her search for the motorcycle.

Getting rid of him wasn't that easy. He insisted on coming up to her room and then wanted to come in. Echo opened the door just a crack, peeked inside, then shook her head. "You can't come in. Trixie's asleep." Actually, Trixie wasn't even there but Pruitt didn't know that.

Clearly disappointed and annoyed, he finally agreed to leave. He didn't try to kiss her. If he had, Echo was positive she would have lost it altogether and smashed in his face. As he turned away, he said cheerfully, "See you tomorrow. And don't go riding in any red Miatas, okay? I wouldn't like that."

How could he be so casual? He had murdered two people that day, coldly and deliberately, and yet there he was telling her good-bye the way almost anyone would tell someone good-bye. Except for the threat about the red Miata.

She had to stop him. Somehow, she had to stop Pruitt.

She waited a safe fifteen minutes to make sure he was gone, armed herself with a flashlight, and slipped out of the empty room to begin her hunt.

Chapter 9

The library book in Pruitt's room that had caught Echo's attention was a volume titled *The Caves of Twin Falls*. Everyone knew the hill on the far side of the old railroad bridge crossing the Salem River behind campus was dotted with caves, large and small. The bridge was supposedly off limits to all students because of its state of disrepair, a rule generally ignored by all but the most timid souls. The rickety old bridge was the fastest, easiest way to get to the woods and caves on the other side, and almost no one had the patience to take the long way around via the river road. Echo had crossed the bridge more than once, but she had never explored the caves.

She was about to remedy that situation now, late on this cool, moonless, Sunday night.

Maybe Pruitt *was* just writing a report on those old caves, Echo told herself as, flashlight off, she hurried across campus toward the river. But if he wasn't, then he had to have another reason for having that book in his room. Wouldn't one of the larger caves be a great place to hide something as big as that motorcycle? Getting it across the bridge without falling through one of the holes in the flooring could be a problem, and hauling it up the hill through the woods to the caves wouldn't be a picnic, either. But if you were determined . . .

Pruitt certainly seemed determined. Not to mention heartless. Poor Polk and Nancy! And Lily was going to be paralyzed if she lived. Pruitt hadn't blinked an eye when he heard that. No sudden flush of guilt had crossed his pale features. He hadn't even stammered when he'd made that crude, unnecessary remark.

Echo's blood chilled anew, thinking of the total lack of emotion Pruitt had displayed upon hearing the news about those two kids on the cliff, too. They were *dead*. Didn't he feel *anything*? Had he hated Nancy that much for dumping him?

Then what would he do to someone who turned him in to the police?

Echo Glenn's life wouldn't be worth two cents.

Cursing the day she had gone to Pruitt and

asked for that bike ride, Echo flicked on the flashlight as she neared the bridge. The sudden, yellowish beam made her uneasy. It wasn't likely that anyone would be on the riverbank this late on a Sunday night, but you never knew. If someone saw her light and came out to check, how would she ever come up with an explanation for being there herself?

Hastily concocting a story about "research for a paper," Echo kept going.

The bridge was in worse shape than she'd remembered. Every step she took brought a screech of protest from the rotting wood beneath her feet. She only weighed a hundred and ten pounds. What kind of noises must the bridge make when Pruitt pushed the heavy motorcycle across it? *If* he had.

She could hear the rushing river far below, and wondered if the water was icy-cold. The nights were still a little cool. Maybe the river hadn't warmed up yet. Not that it made any difference. If the ramshackle wooden walkway beneath her opened up suddenly and she plummeted to the river below, she'd drown no matter what the water temperature was. She wasn't a good enough swimmer to fight that vicious current.

Clutching the decrepit wooden railing with one hand, the other hand forging a path through the darkness with the flashlight, Echo kept going, walking as lightly as possible.

The bridge seemed miles long.

Finally, she reached the end and rushed off the bridge to stand at the foot of a steep, wooded slope. Shivering in her denim jacket, she glanced around. The hill was a black mound rising up in front of her, covered with towering pine trees, smaller leaf-bearing trees, and thick underbrush. This was unfamiliar territory even in daylight. She felt as if she'd been set down in the middle of a strange planet. And she had no idea which direction to take. Left? Right? Straight up?

Deciding on straight up, she played the flashlight beam ahead of her as she climbed, pushing aside underbrush, her feet sliding occasionally in soft, pine-needled earth. The first cave was much too small to hide anything as huge as the motorcycle. The second was larger, but dark and empty.

When she became tired and discouraged, she focused her thoughts on the two innocent students in the red Miata, and kept going. She imagined the raw terror they must have felt when that car sailed off the edge of the cliff, and that thought forced her feet onward and upward. Someone had to stop Pruitt!

Hating him with a raw, blistering passion,

she slipped and slid and climbed some more and slid again, scraping one hand on a sharp rock, slicing a finger on a thorny bush, and losing several strands of her hair to a prickly pine bough. Still she kept going. When she lost her balance and tumbled sideways, landing at the mouth of another cave, it took her several moments to get her bearings and pull herself upright to wave the flashlight around her.

And there it was.

Black as night, black as death, the motorcycle stood smack in the middle of the low-ceilinged, stone-walled cave.

The motorcycle wasn't the only thing in the cave.

Echo glanced around her at what appeared to be a mini-garage. The motorcycle was surrounded by a large collection of tools, neatly arranged on makeshift "shelves" of flat rocks piled on top of one another. Besides the tools, there were cans of gasoline, piles of jeans and sweatshirts carefully folded and lying on the rock, plus objects that Echo assumed were motorcycle spare parts, and, atop a pile of books in the corner, a handful of newspaper clippings, no doubt Pruitt's press notices about the biker attacks. What an ego!

There were other books, a portable tape player, bags of snack food, and cans of soda.

But it was the motorcycle Echo was most interested in.

She had found it. Here it was, standing right in front of her. Now all she had to do was figure out how to identify it as Pruitt's, and then she could leave, call the police, and direct them to the cave. She wouldn't even have to give her name, wouldn't have to be connected with the discovery at all.

If Pruitt gave *her* name to the police, she'd stonewall it. Lie. He had no proof that she was the one who had joined him on that devastating ride to Johnny's Place. She *hadn't* known what he was going to do, so she wasn't guilty of anything except stupidity. If you went to jail for stupidity, there'd be no room in the prisons for real criminals.

Worst case scenario . . . she'd admit the truth, if she had to. And beg for mercy.

The important thing was, Pruitt would be put away where he couldn't hurt anyone else. Including her.

Before she began looking for something to link Pruitt to the bike, Echo grabbed a large knife with a wickedly sharp blade from the makeshift shelves. He probably used it to open cans. *She* was going to use it to open tires.

Echo attacked the tires with the knife until both tires were in shreds and the air had hissed out angrily. Echo dropped the knife and began hunting for something that would absolutely link Pruitt to the bike. The license plates wouldn't help, she thought, since he had said the bike wasn't registered in his name. They would prove that the bike had been stolen, but not who had stolen it. There had to be something in all this junk, something that would hang him.

What? She didn't even know what to look for.

She was leafing through the textbooks on the shelves, looking for Pruitt's name or student I.D. number, when she heard a sound outside the cave.

Echo's head flew up. Bats? Oh, God, they didn't live in *here*, did they? They weren't about to return to their home for the night, were they?

The sound came again. Too heavy to be the fluttering of a bat's wings. It sounded far more human than that. Footsteps, plodding up the steep, slippery slope. Human footsteps.

Someone was coming. Walking with purpose, toward the cave.

Only one person would be coming to this cave so late at night.

Pruitt.

Pruitt was coming to the cave to check on

his motorcycle, the way some farmers checked on their livestock one last time before going to bed.

Echo glanced around frantically. She couldn't let him find her here, especially now that she'd savaged his beloved bike.

But there was nowhere to hide.

Whistling . . . he was whistling. As if he hadn't a worry in the world.

Unlike her.

Eyes wide with terror, Echo scuttled backward, into the darkest depths of the cave, looking for a way out.

There was none. The cave had no rear exit. It narrowed gradually and then became solid rock wall.

Although she needed the flashlight, she had no choice. He was getting too close. She flicked off the beam.

Crablike, she slid sideways in her desperation, hoping to find some small cubbyhole, even the narrowest of openings to disappear into. When Pruitt saw that bike, realized that someone had been here, he would explode in rage. If he found her, she would become the target of that rage.

There! A tiny, narrow crevasse in the wall, behind her. Even as the heavy footsteps arrived at the mouth of the cave, Echo held her breath and squeezed her long, thin form in between the two walls of the opening. Icy, spring-fed water trickled down from the ceiling, dripping slowly onto her scalp. She had scraped the skin on both arms squeezing her way in, and now, wedged against the stone as if they'd been nailed there, they burned painfully.

Her breath came with difficulty. Her teeth bit into the soft flesh of her lower lip to keep from screaming as she visualized Pruitt standing in the mouth of the cave looking at the ruin of his most prized possession.

The sound she had so dreaded came no more than a second or two later. It was a shout so filled with rage and fury it stopped her heart.

At that very second, trapped in her narrow, stone-cold hideaway, her arms squeezed against her sides, her legs aching with the painful confinement, icy water dripping onto her scalp, Echo Glenn knew as surely as she knew her own name that she would never leave the cave alive.

Chapter 10

Echo knew she should stay completely hidden, knew that her very life depended on remaining totally invisible. But she couldn't help it. When the first bellow of wild rage was followed immediately by a second and then a third, and she could hear stomping sounds and banging sounds and crashing sounds, she had to look. Not knowing what was happening was unbearable.

Her head with its thick hair was solidly wedged in between the two slabs of rock that made up her prison. She had to push with her back and shoulders to slip free just enough to make peering around the edge of her stone wall possible. She was careful to keep the rest of herself hidden.

A lantern with a garish yellow glow had been set against one wall, bathing the interior of the cave with light. What Echo saw in that light was terrifying.

The leather-clad figure in the shiny black helmet and plastic face shield had gone mad with rage over the damage done to the motorcycle. The screaming and shouting of foul obscenities wasn't enough to placate him. To better demonstrate his fury, he was snatching up one tool after another from the stone shelves and heaving them at the walls. Some broke upon impact and fell to the ground like broken toys. Others remained intact, bouncing away from the wall to litter the floor of the cave. His rage kept him from standing still. He was jumping up and down in a mad dance like a marionette on strings. Spinning around, arms waving, feet kicking out. He shouted, he screamed, he threw things against the wall.

At one point in his terrifying demonstration of unbridled fury, he danced precariously close to Echo's hideaway.

She froze, whisked her head back in, scraping the side of one cheek, and remained there, shaking with fear, until, still screaming and shouting, he had danced away again.

This was a whole different side of Pruitt that she was seeing. She had hated the cold, calculating Pruitt, but that dispassionate, heartless side of him hadn't paralyzed her with fear as much as this deranged, demented side of him did. Maybe there was a slight chance that you could reason with the dispassionate Pruitt. Maybe if she had been able to say to him that night in front of Johnny's Place, "Don't do this, Pruitt, you'll be sorry," and if he could have heard her words over the roar of the motorcycle, maybe he would have steered around those people. The possibility, she knew, was remote, but it could be there.

But there would be *no* reasoning with this incoherent, irrational madman running around the cave, ranting and raving, flinging tools and books and canned goods at the stone walls.

If he found her now, she was dead.

She should have kept the knife she'd used on the tires.

The screaming stopped, not suddenly, but slowly, dwindling to an angry mutter. The clanging against the wall ceased a moment later.

Echo worked up enough courage to glance over the edge of her wall again.

He had his back to her, and was dragging two tires over to the motorcycle, muttering the whole time.

Echo strained to listen.

"Lousy vandals, think they're going to stop

me." Mutter, mutter . . . "Touching my things, my private property, who do they think they are? They'll be sorry." Mutter, mutter. He removed the ruined rear tire, replacing it quickly with the new one.

Dismayed, Echo watched in silence. He wasn't going to take the bike, was he? That would ruin everything! She'd have nothing then to take to the police, except the location of the cave. And what good would that do her without the motorcycle itself?

"It'd take more than two ruined tires to stop me now. It's been going so well, exactly the way I wanted. Almost finished, not quite . . ." Mutter, mutter.

Echo struggled to hear. Almost finished with what? Changing the tires? Or something else? Something much more . . . deadly? He was making so much noise, clattering and clanking as he dropped one tool and picked up another, she could barely hear.

He kept his back to her, almost as if he knew she was there. But she knew he didn't. He had lifted the face shield, but was still wearing the helmet, which made her heart sink. He'd have taken it off if he wasn't planning, at any moment, to ride the bike right out of the cave. And there was no way she could stop him. Wouldn't even dare try. It would be safer for her if he was never, for one moment, aware of her presence in the cave.

"I'm not stopping until I get what I want, and no one can make me stop. I didn't come all this way for nothing." The new front tire was in place. He stood up, dusting off his gloved hand with satisfaction.

"Shouldn't have touched my bike." The voice was cold, hard, and angry. *"Isn't that how all of this started? Someone who shouldn't have been anywhere near a motorcycle was allowed to touch it. And nothing was ever the same again after that."*

With that final, cryptic comment, the lantern went out, plunging the cave into complete darkness. A second later, the bike's engine roared to life.

When Echo peeked out again from behind the stone wall, she felt, rather than saw, that she was alone in the cave. Pruitt and the motorcycle were gone.

She stayed in the crevasse another agonizingly painful few minutes, just to make sure. The top of her head was icy cold and very wet, and her arms and legs and hips burned from being squeezed between the layers of rock. But if she moved out into the mouth of the cave and he was still sitting right outside, he'd see her. She'd never get away from him then.

She tilted her head, listening. There it was, the faint roar of the bike, fading further and further away.

He *was* gone.

With effort, she pushed herself free of the stone walls and, rubbing her scraped elbows to soothe them, moved back into the middle of the cave, stumbling over the mess now littering the floor. It was late. He wouldn't be gone long. He'd be back to put the bike to bed for the night, and she didn't dare be here when he returned. There was no time to search for something that would associate Pruitt with the hideaway.

Where was her flashlight? Taking the time to hunt for it could mean the difference between making it back to the dorm in safety or getting caught for a second time that night. And taking the lantern with her would be foolish. If she did run into him, she could lie about where she'd been. But not with his lantern in her hands.

She would have to go back in the dark.

The thought that she had risked her life for nothing was galling. Desperate, Echo bent to fumble around in the dark for something, anything, to take with her. She grabbed the first thing her fingers touched. It felt like a notebook with a hard cover. Maybe it was something, maybe it wasn't. But she wasn't leaving empty-handed. Not after what she'd been through.

She thrust the notebook into the waistband of her jeans and, turned and hurried from the cave.

The hike back to campus was a nerve-wracking one. Sliding down the alternately rocky, then slippery, hill was much harder without the aid of a light. With no moon above, she couldn't see a thing but black, bulky shadows. Worse, she couldn't be sure Pruitt wasn't hiding somewhere, behind a boulder or a bush, waiting to see if the culprit who had ruined his tires was still hanging around. She stayed within the shelter of the pine trees and the undergrowth as much as possible, glancing over her shoulder repeatedly. Twice she fell, tripping over a large rock or a fallen tree limb. Both times she scrambled upward quickly, afraid that if she remained on the ground, an angry Pruitt would suddenly appear from behind one of the bushes, pounce on her like a cougar, and choke the life out of her.

Crossing the railroad bridge was the worst. If he came roaring out of the darkness on his way back to the cave while she was on the bridge, where would she hide? There was no place for her to go, unless she was willing to dive into the cold, rushing waters below. I might have some tiny little chance against him, she told herself as she hurried across the creaking bridge, but I'd have no chance against the river.

She stayed as close to the railing as possible, ears alert for any sound of an approaching motorcycle.

It never came.

She made it back to Lester without incident.

Only to find her room crowded with Trixie's "study group."

Echo heard the girls before she got to the door, and groaned aloud. She'd forgotten it was Sunday night. Every Sunday, Trixie and her pals, which included Deejay, Marilyn, and Ruthanne and a bunch of other girls Echo didn't know and had no desire to know, went to the movie in the rec center and then returned to room 324 at Lester to "study." Echo usually escaped to the library long before the group arrived.

But tonight, all she wanted to do was take a hot shower and crawl into bed. She needed peace and privacy to decide what to do about the cave. There'd be no peace or privacy in her room tonight.

She was surprised to find the room unusually

quiet when she opened the door and walked in. They were all there, sprawling on the floor or sitting on Trixie's bed (not on hers, Echo noticed gratefully), but the usual loud music was absent, no one was laughing, and even the conversation seemed subdued.

"Wow, what happened to you?" Trixie cried when Echo walked in and plopped down on her bed: "I thought you had a date. You look like you've been mud-wrestling instead. I told you you were nuts, going out with someone like Pruitt. He's too weird."

"Hey," Deejay protested. "Pruitt's not nuts! He's just . . . different, that's all. You don't even know him, Trixie. Leave Echo alone."

"I don't want to know him," Trixie said. "And I don't understand why Echo *does*."

"I wasn't with Pruitt," Echo said wearily. "The date ended a long time ago. I went for a walk and I . . . I fell."

No one seemed to care where Echo had been, and Trixie went on to explain, "We were just talking about those two kids in the Miata. The car that went over the cliff? Polk Malone and Nancy Becker. No classes tomorrow, because of them. Marilyn said the dean's going ballistic, because she's had to field a lot of phone calls from parents about the Mad Biker."

The topic of conversation explained why they were all so unusually quiet. It was a depressing subject.

"Well, if Nancy Becker had kept dating Pruitt," Deejay said, "she wouldn't be dead now, would she?"

You don't know how right you are, Echo thought bitterly. She knew Deejay meant that Nancy would have been with Pruitt, instead of in Polk's car. She didn't mean that if Nancy hadn't dumped Pruitt, she'd still be alive.

Echo went into the bathroom, closed the door, and sank down on the floor with her head in her hands. She was going to have to keep seeing Pruitt, horrible though the thought was, until she had something to take to the police. And not just because she wanted, needed, to prove him guilty. Because she feared for her very life. Ignoring Pruitt's threats would be foolish, even crazy.

When she came out of the bathroom, Ruthanne was saying vehemently, "Well, somebody has to do something! Everyone's scared to death. It could be any one of us next time. People are going to start hiding in their rooms pretty soon."

"I agree with Deejay," Marilyn said quietly. "At least Echo won't be alone like she usually is. She has Pruitt to keep an eye on her now."

That was so close to what Pruitt was actually doing, Echo fought an urge to laugh aloud. She was tired, and scared, and sick at heart. Unless that notebook she'd taken from the cave proved valuable, she'd wasted two hours when she should have been studying for finals, and she had almost been caught by an insane killer in the process. "That part about hiding in our rooms," she said, not caring if she was being rude, "sounds like a great idea. Since you guys aren't really doing anything here, maybe you could go back to your rooms and do nothing, okay? I need to sleep."

No one took offense. It was late and they were all still shaken by the afternoon's tragedy. They left quietly.

When they had gone, Echo took a hot shower and crawled into bed, tired and aching.

But she didn't go to sleep right away. Two people had been killed today, brutally, in what looked like a random, vicious act of cruelty.

And she, Echo Glenn, knew who had done it. She couldn't prove it, not yet, but she knew.

Ruthanne, for once, was right. Somebody had to do *something*.

There had to be some way to prove what Echo Glenn knew about Aaron Pruitt.

Checking first to make sure the deep, even

breathing coming from Trixie's bed meant that she really was sound asleep, Echo reached under her pillow and pulled forth the black notebook she had surreptitiously slipped beneath it when she'd flopped down on her bed earlier.

Switching on the small blue lamp on her bedside table, she began reading.

Chapter 11

The entries in the journal weren't dated. The handwriting was barely legible, and there weren't many entries. The first was brief, but bitter:

Everything is ruined. Everything! No reason to live now. Life will never be good again, like it was. Can't be. It's not fair. Not fair!

The second entry was angrier, less despairing: *Why should I stop living? I haven't done anything wrong. It wasn't my fault. It was someone else's. That's who should die, not me. But it shouldn't be a quick, painless death. It should be slow and torturous, deservedly so. Like Ross's. His death wasn't quick and painless. Far from it. He was dragged such a long way, his skin being ripped off by the highway, his clothes shredded. I thought he would never stop screaming. I'll hear those screams in my sleep until the day I die. But then when the screaming stopped, I wanted it to start again so that I would know he was still alive.*

But he wasn't.

I couldn't go to him, couldn't help him. I wanted to, but I couldn't. My legs wouldn't work, and there was a bone sticking out of my right arm. Even now, weeks later, I'm having trouble writing this.

Whatever sentence the judge pronounces, it won't be harsh enough. Can't be. I wish I could be the one to decide what the punishment should be.

The third entry was frightening in its rage:

The judge said "Accidental death!" I can't believe it!

The judge was wrong. There wasn't anything accidental about it. It was negligence, pure and simple. Criminal negligence. Ross took the bike in to have it fixed, not to have it destroyed. He thought it had been put back together the way it was supposed to be. He didn't know the clerk had messed up, forgotten to order the right part. Afraid to admit it. So a part found in the back of the shop was substituted. But that part was back there because it was defective! It had been taken off another bike. The clerk never checked. Neither did the mechanic, because he thought it was the new part that was supposed to have been ordered.

That's what killed Ross. They gave him back his bike with a defective part, all because of that spineless clerk. If that isn't negligence, I don't know what is. Like I said, criminal negligence!

Mom said when she looked up, toward the front of the room, she thought she saw a smile on the face of the person who had trashed our lives forever. A smile! Well, why not? Justice wasn't being served, was it? There wasn't going to be any punishment, none at all, so why not smile?

She said it was all she could do to keep from rushing up there and smashing in that face.

If the law isn't going to seek justice, I'll have to. I have no choice. This crime can't go unpunished. That wouldn't be right. It would make a mockery of Ross's death. I can't sit by and let that happen.

And I won't. I promised Ross. We went to the cemetery a couple of weeks later. Mom cried her eyes out and Dad just kept quiet.

Mom and Dad left and I was alone with him, and I knelt beside the grave. That's when I promised Ross. "It wasn't an accident," I told him. "You and I both know that. I'm going to see to it that you didn't die for nothing, Ross. I promise." Then I stuck the flowers I had brought him into the dirt, and went to the car.

Now all I have to figure out is how to keep my promise.

There was one last entry in the black notebook:

It's been a long, hot summer and it hasn't been easy, but I made it. I spent a lot of long, painful hours thinking and planning, and I've already started acting out my long-term plan. I think it will work.

I bought the clerk's bike. Hadn't ridden it much, anyway, just enough to put on an act for a while. It didn't work. Nobody bought the new image. Of course it was for sale. Who would want to keep it after what happened? It took every ounce of courage I had to even touch it. But I knew I had to. The garage owner looked so surprised when I walked in and asked about the bike. I could tell he thought I should be the last person in the world to buy a motorcycle. Especially that one. I didn't care what he thought.

I'm teaching myself to ride it. It's hard, and it hurts. But I keep thinking about Ross, and I know this is something I have to do. And I'm getting pretty good. I keep the bike hidden, so my parents won't know. They're so wrecked, they don't know or care where I am half the time, anyway. I only ride at night, when it's dark, on back roads where no one can see me.

Not that anyone would ever believe it's me. Still, there's no point in taking chances. Wouldn't want to spoil everything before my plan even gets off the ground.

Sometimes when I'm riding, I see it all happening again: Ross picking me up after school because Mom had a committee meeting. Ross teasing me because I had sworn I would never, ever climb on that monster of a bike. Then the speed and the power of it took over, and I actually relaxed. I was hanging on him like mad, but I was enjoying the wind in my face and the feeling that was so much like flying.

And then something went terribly wrong and I knew it had gone terribly wrong because the bike sort of flew up into the air and Ross screamed and then I screamed and then the bike landed and tipped over on its side and I was thrown free but Ross was trapped somehow alongside the bike and it kept skidding and sliding, really fast along the rough surface of the road with him being dragged along beside it, his clothes were shredding, and he was screaming for someone to help him but I couldn't move, I couldn't . . .

Reading, Echo shuddered at the very vivid image the words conjured up.

I will have scars inside and out that will never go away.

But I mustn't think about that now. I have to push those thoughts away and keep practicing, practicing, until I'm as good as Ross was. Then I can do anything I want. Then I can keep my promise to Ross.

There were no more entries in the book.

Echo closed it, slid it back underneath her pillow, and lay down, no longer aware of her painful scrapes and bruises. Something had gone wrong. Pruitt had been riding a motorcycle with . . . who? A best friend? A cousin, a brother? And something had gone wrong, something a judge had called "accidental," but Pruitt had not. And now he was out for revenge? Unless she had read wrong, he was now using a bike that had belonged to the clerk whose negligence had killed someone. Had bought it and taught himself to ride it, always with a plan in mind. That seemed pretty sick to her.

Scary. That much rage, that much determination, was very scary. How could she possibly fight that?

Pruitt was on a mission. It was very clear from the notebook that he didn't intend to let anyone or anything stand in his way. He had already killed. He wouldn't hesitate to kill again. And he certainly wouldn't hesitate to kill anyone who tried to stop him.

Echo closed her eyes and rolled over on her side, facing the wall. What did the old woman and the little boy in town, the shoppers at the mall, the group in front of Johnny's Place and those two freshmen in the red Miata have to do with the death of Ross? They couldn't possibly all have been involved, could they? Pruitt wasn't even *from* Twin Falls. She had seen him arrive on campus in late August flanked by a trunk and two suitcases. He couldn't be a townie. So why attack the townspeople?

Pruitt isn't sane, Echo, she told herself. You must know that by now. So quit looking for logical explanations. Pruitt didn't go after those people because of Ross. He went after them because he *wanted* to, because he doesn't know what he's doing anymore. Maybe he did start out with a plan, like the notebook says. But he must have abandoned it when insanity took over.

There was no name in or on the notebook, no way of connecting it to Pruitt. Handwriting, maybe . . . an expert would be able to match the entries with Pruitt's penmanship. But she couldn't very well go to the police and ask them to test Pruitt's handwriting. Nothing in the notebook identified him as the Mad Biker.

Two things might hang him. The motorcycle, for one. If she sent the police to the cave, they could probably link the bike to Aaron Pruitt somehow. Second, the notebook, *if* she could first make sure that Pruitt really had had a friend or relative named Ross. That was probably something she should do *before* she called the police, otherwise the notebook would be worthless.

She couldn't very well come right out and ask Pruitt about someone named Ross. He had already threatened her. Her life wouldn't be worth spit if he knew she had that notebook.

She'd figure out what to do. Because Ruthanne was right. Two more people were dead and someone had to *do* something. She was the only one on campus who knew the identity of the Mad Biker, so that someone would have to be her.

Chapter 12

On Monday morning, Echo had to fight the urge to call the police and direct them to the cave. Without something to tie Pruitt to the bike, some tiny piece of evidence that he had staked out that cave for his own use, the phone call would be a waste of time.

So she fought against the sense of urgency that was tying her stomach in knots, brought on by fear that at any second, the biker would strike again. If one more person died or was maimed when she already *knew* who the guilty party was, she wouldn't be able to live with her guilt.

She turned on the radio, half-expecting to hear another horror story about an attack during the night. She had seen with her own eyes Pruitt taking the bike from the cave in an enraged state. What mayhem had he wreaked this time?

But there was nothing, except an announcement that classes had been cancelled out of respect for Polk Malone and Nancy Becker.

A rap song with a great beat in the background took over the air waves and Echo heaved a huge sigh of relief. The Mad Biker hadn't struck again. Maybe knowing that someone had found his cave and was aware of his hiding-place was worrying him, forcing him to play it safe for a little while. That would be good. It would give her a little breathing room, maybe even enough time to link him to the notebook and the cave and the bike so she could go to the police.

There might be a way. The infirmary had in its files medical histories of every student on campus. Providing a medical history was required of all incoming freshmen. Upon admission last August, Echo had had to list every member of her immediate family, living or deceased, and mention whether or not they had any physical condition worth noting, or cause of death. Since "abandonment of child" wasn't among the ailments listed, she had answered most of the questions in the negative, except for her grandfather's diabetes and her grandmother's heart condition.

She thought of those forms now. Pruitt must have filled one out, too. If the "Ross" mentioned in the notebook had been a close relative, and he must have been or his parents wouldn't have been so devastated, Pruitt would have had to list him, adding that he was deceased and giving the cause of death. If she could locate Pruitt's medical file, find the name "Ross" listed there, she could make a copy of it, using it to connect Pruitt to the notebook, and, therefore, to the bike in the cave.

Dressing quickly in jeans and an oversized Salem U sweatshirt and sneakers, Echo hurried off to the infirmary. If anyone asked, she could simply say that since there were no classes that day, she'd decided to earn a few extra bucks. No one would question that. If it wasn't busy, she'd have all the time in the world to look for Pruitt's file.

It wasn't busy. Everyone was taking advantage of the nice weather and the day off to do things far more fun than running to the infirmary for medical advice.

She was just bending over the metal drawer labelled "P-R" in the empty file room when a voice from the doorway said, "They let *you* work here? Someone with a profound disregard for human life? Aren't they worried about being sued for reckless endangerment?"

Echo flew upright, her cheeks burning, her

hands flying away from the metal drawer as if it had just bitten her.

Liam McCullough, his left wrist in a cast and a nasty bruise over one eye, was leaning against the open door. Dark auburn hair curled across his forehead and down the back of his neck, and his arms and legs in shorts and a Salem T-shirt were deeply tanned.

"Don't you believe in knocking?" she said sharply, annoyed with him for catching her off-guard. And for *almost* catching her in the act of snooping.

One dark eyebrow lifted to meet the bruise. "Well, it's not like you were treating a patient in here." An expression of mock horror crossed his strong-boned, tanned face. "They *don't* let you treat patients, do they?"

Echo didn't answer. The cold metal of the file drawer was burning a hole in her back. Her fingers were itching to get to it. What was he doing in here, anyway? This wasn't a treatment room.

To her dismay, he moved into the room, stopping just a few feet short of where she stood with her back to the file cabinet. His eyes, she couldn't help noticing, were not pale and expressionless like Pruitt's. They were light brown, almost amber. "So, is that what you were doing when you attacked me on the river path with your bike?" he asked. "Drumming up patients for this place? You have to go out and drag them in here, is that it?"

Although his tone of voice wasn't angry, but cautiously friendly, Echo's pulse skipped a beat, wondering briefly if he really *was* talking about the incident on the river path. Maybe he wasn't. Maybe he suspected that she had been on the motorcycle in front of Johnny's Place and he was testing, waiting to see her reaction to his comments.

Well, he wasn't going to get a rise out of her. "That was an accident," she said, her voice smooth as pudding. "I told you that at the time. I didn't *see* you. And you shouldn't have jumped out of the woods like that without looking to see if anyone was coming."

To her surprise, he nodded. "Right. You are right. I was thinking about a paper I had to write, forty percent of my final grade in psych, and I wasn't my usual alert self." He grinned. "I'll forgive you if you'll forgive me."

Feeling uncertain, Echo nodded. What was he doing here? What did he *want*?

He got right to it. "Saw you with Pruitt at the movie last night." He shook his head. "He doesn't seem like your type."

"You couldn't possibly have the faintest notion what my type is," Echo said archly. If he didn't leave soon, someone would come into the room to work and then she'd never get to that file. "You don't know anything about me."

"That's true. But that's only because everyone I asked said you were a loner. That you wouldn't be interested in seeing a movie with me or going boating on the river or dancing at Johnny's Place. That's why I was so surprised to see you walk into the rec center last night with Pruitt."

He had asked people about her? Before or after she'd clobbered him with her bike?

"I mean," he went on, resting the injured wrist on the top of a metal file cabinet next to him, "if you were going to go to a movie with anyone, it should have been me, not Pruitt. You owe me for ruining my run that day. Unless, of course, he was just another one of your victims."

She bit back the words, "Actually, it's the other way around. I'm one of *his* victims." It struck her then as bitterly ironic that Liam was joking about people being hit by bikes at a time when people had *died* after being struck by a bike. A different kind of bike, true, and she could see that he wasn't making the connection, but still . . .

"Well, he wasn't one of my victims," she answered, "but I . . . I did owe him something, in a way."

He looked interested: "So you two aren't an item?"

Echo shook her head vigorously. Maybe too vigorously, she realized then, remembering that Pruitt had promised they'd be seeing more of each other. Liam seemed nice enough, now that he didn't hate her any more. But this was no time to get someone involved in the mess she was in. Pruitt had made some nasty threat about "competition." Look what he'd done to Polk Malone.

"Look, I'm very busy here," she said, meaning it because, right now, she wanted nothing more than to get her hands on Pruitt's medical file. It suddenly seemed like the most important thing in the world. And Liam was in the way. "I don't want to be rude, but . . ."

The high, angled cheekbones flushed slightly. His arm came off the file cabinet and he stood up straight. "So they were right about you, I guess," he said, his voice gone flat. "You really are a loner. Except for Pruitt, of course." He turned away, headed for the door. "Actually," he said over his shoulder, "I came in to have my cast checked and got the wrong room. Sorry I bothered you." Then he was gone.

He did seem nice. Odd-colored eyes. Kind of like a cat's. But warm.

If he'd gotten run over by that motorcycle, like Lily D'Agostino, those eyes would be cold and empty, like a house with no one home.

Echo turned back to the "P-R" file drawer, wrapped her fingers around the brass pull, yanked, and almost wailed aloud with disappointment.

The drawer was locked.

Well, of *course* it's locked, she told herself, sagging against the cabinet. Those files are confidential. Did you really expect the drawers to be unlocked so that anyone who chose to could waltz right in and read medical files?

Disheartened, she decided she might just as well leave the infirmary. It wasn't busy, she wasn't really needed, and she wasn't going to learn anything useful. Maybe if she sneaked back up to the cave, she could do a more thorough search, come up with something incriminating.

She glanced at her watch. Almost noon. The day was speeding by and so far, she hadn't accomplished a thing. Tomorrow, she'd have classes most of the day, and work.

And by tomorrow, someone else could be dead.

She was halfway back to Lester to change

into boots for the climb up the hill to the cave when someone called out to her. She turned, half-expecting to see Deejay or Marilyn waving.

Pruitt. Running toward her across campus.

Her heart sank. He'd blackmail her into spending the afternoon with him, and she'd never get near the cave.

Inspiration struck. If she *had* to be with Pruitt, she'd use the time well.

Slightly out of breath, he caught up with her. "Boating," he said. "We're going boating on the river. And don't give me any excuses. I've already made plans."

"Okay," Echo said blithely, "why not? Such a gorgeous day. But first, I have to make a quick phone call. You don't mind waiting, do you? It'll only take a minute."

"Make it quick," he ordered, his normal breathing restored, taking her elbow to propel her across the sprawling green lawn. "Who you calling?"

They passed the fountain on the Commons. Echo was vaguely aware of Liam McCullough's large form sprawled on the low stone wall, sensed that he looked up as she passed with Pruitt. No time to think about that now. She had more important things on her mind.

It was very important that she have a clear

view of Pruitt's face as she answered his question. Her head turned, her eyes focused clearly, and she said, "I have to call my brother. My older brother." She had no brothers and no sisters, but he couldn't know that. "We're very close. He's helping me through school, and I call him every week."

"Didn't know you had a brother. What's his name?"

Echo went in for the kill. Never taking her eyes from his face for a second, she said proudly, "Ross. His name is Ross, and he's really cool."

She didn't know what she had expected, but she wasn't prepared for Pruitt's reaction. He drew in his breath in a shocked gasp, every last ounce of color drained from his face and he stopped short, stumbling and almost falling. When he recovered his balance, he hissed in Echo's face, "What did you say?"

If Echo had had any doubt at all that the notebook she'd taken from the cave belonged to Pruitt, it disintegrated under the force of his reaction. It was perfectly clear that the name "Ross" shattered him.

Frightened by the strength of his reaction and wondering if she'd overplayed her hand, Echo backtracked. "Well, his name isn't really Ross," she amended, her voice still light, and remarkably steady. "It's actually John Ross. But since my dad has the same name and everyone calls him John, we call my brother Ross. Easier that way." She looked up at Pruitt with deliberately innocent eyes. "Don't you think?"

The color returned to his face in a flood and she could almost smell the relief. "Oh," he breathed heavily, "oh, *John* Ross." Then he began babbling, "John Ross, yeah, nice name, didn't know you had a brother, nice of him to help you out with school . . ."

Echo wasn't listening. She had found out what she needed to know.

Now all she had to do was decide what to do with it. Before someone else died.

Chapter 13

A tall brunette named Gabriella Stone raced along the river path, ponytail bouncing on the back of her neck as she ran. Her dirty white sneakers barely touched the ground as she went, and her white shorts and tank top were wet with sweat. The sun was hot, the air very still and thickening with humidity, but she never slackened her pace. Her feet, pumping as steadily as her strong, healthy heart, left a fine spray of dirt in their wake.

Gabriella's concentration was so great, she didn't hear the motorcycle until it was almost on top of her. It came roaring not straight down the path behind her, but out of the woods, leaping over a growth of underbrush like a stunt cycle in an adventure movie, landing sideways on the path with a bone-shaking thud fifty feet behind the runner.

Crying out in surprise, she spun around, her

lips forming the word, "What . . . ?" Then her expression changed from bewilderment to fear as she realized what she was looking at. Her eyes said quite clearly that she remembered, then, exactly *how* that red Miata had gone sailing off the overlook. Her deeply tanned face went as white as her tank top and her eyes widened in dread. "You . . ." she whispered to the leather jacket and shiny black helmet and custom-made boots, "you . . . !"

The engine purred for another second or two, and then a black-booted foot pushed down on a pedal, black-gloved hands twisted near the handlebars, revving the engine, and the bike began moving.

But . . . it moved slowly, this time, leisurely, as if it intended only to peacefully accompany the girl as she completed her run. They might have been two people out for a companionable stroll along the riverbank, one on foot, the other on an ambling motorcycle.

Confused, Gabriella kept her eyes on the biker, so close to her now that she could clearly see the intricate, colored pattern on the boots. She took a step backward, then another, until her shoulders collided with the trunk of a tree lining the path. "What do you want?" she breathed, frightened to the core by the forboding figure. Black helmet. Dark, smoke-colored face shield hiding even his eyes from her. Black clothing, head to toe, black gloves hiding his hands from her. And the bike itself, the growling monster aimed straight at her, was black as coal. "Go away! Leave me alone!"

The bike stopped, its engine murmuring softly. One booted foot came off the pedal and rested on the path again.

The girl glanced around frantically, up the path toward school and back down it again, the way she had come. There was no one. Only the biker.

"You could," a voice said softly from behind the face shield, "run for the river. You're fast. You might get by me and dive into the water before I could stop you. But you'd probably drown. That current is deadly. Or you could try the woods, if a swim isn't what you had in mind. But this baby," patting the handlebars affectionately, "can go anywhere. Uphill, downhill, on rough terrain, doesn't matter. And it's faster than you've ever dreamed of running, Gabriella."

The girl shrank against the tree. She swallowed hard. Her dark eyes in the ghostly-pale face were round with terror. "I haven't done anything to you," she whispered.

The black helmet nodded. "This is true." The

foot returned to the pedal. "But then, you're not going to die because of something *you* did. You're going to die because of something someone *else* did." He shook his head ruefully. "Not fair, I know. But then, hell, what is?"

Gabriella tried to digest his words. Die? She was going to die? He didn't really mean that, did he? He had killed others, she knew that. But they weren't *her*. She couldn't die. Not now, not today, not yet! She had never even thought about dying until she'd heard about Polk and Nancy. And to be honest, she hadn't thought about it that long then, because after all, it wasn't *her*.

She was too young to die.

But then, Polk and Nancy hadn't been any older than she was.

He couldn't mean it. He *couldn't*. She wouldn't *let* him kill her. He had no right. No right at all.

The trained athlete in her took over. Her adrenaline pumping, she threw her shoulders back and raised her chin defiantly. She was suddenly very angry with herself for the wimpish way she had spoken to him. She was *not* going to die! Not today. Not at *his* hands. And she wasn't going to get on her knees and beg, either. It probably wouldn't do any good anyway.

Her eyes darted to the river. The water looked cold, and he was probably right about the current. She had heard that it was horrendous. Even if she was willing to try it, she'd never make it past the bike. It barred her way, a solid black wall between her and the river.

The woods? What were her chances of darting into the woods and zigzagging fast enough that she'd lose him?

Nil. She knew that. Knew it as surely and sickeningly as she knew she should have listened to the security guard who had called after her as she began her run, "I wouldn't be running alone just now, Miss. That biker's still out there somewhere."

Why hadn't she listened?

Because until now, until this minute, Gabriella Stone had never been afraid of anything.

She was afraid now. And he *knew* it. She wished, passionately, that she hadn't allowed him to see that.

Maybe if she fought back, she'd have a chance. Maybe all he was really trying to do was scare her half to death. They weren't up on the overlook where the Miata had been parked, they were much closer to campus. Pretty risky to kill someone *here*. If she gave him a hard time, maybe he'd give up and let her go. He *was* just a coward, after all, or he wouldn't need the bike to do his dirty work for him.

She was *not* going down without a fight. "You *hide* behind that bike!" she said with a contemptuous sneer. "Like some lowlife criminal hiding behind a gun. Without that gun, he's nothing and he knows it. The same goes for you. Without that bike, I'll bet you're nothing!"

Although his foot returned to the pedal and he revved the engine, he seemed to hesitate.

That moment's hesitation was just long enough for Gabriella to convince herself that she'd taken the right approach, that fighting him was her way out, after all. He hadn't expected any trouble from her, had he? Thought it would be so easy, her out here alone on this path, him on that powerful motorcycle. Well, he wasn't so sure now, was he? Any second now, if she stood her ground, he'd give up, turn that horrible bike around, and take it and himself out of her sight.

She wasn't going to die today, after all.

Gabriella began shouting at him again, her voice louder and stronger than before.

She was still shouting when the bike roared straight at her and slammed her against the tree, crushing her instantly.

Then the biker drove slowly, nonchalantly, up the path toward campus.

Leaving no one behind to tell the world that when Gabriella Stone died at the hands of the Mad Biker, she was not on her knees begging for mercy.

Chapter 14

Echo got rid of Pruitt by faking a sudden head-ache. He wasn't happy about it but he was still too rattled by the name "Ross" to put up much of an argument.

When he had gone, Echo hurried to her room.

Trixie was there. Burning with impatience, Echo had to wait until Deejay, Marilyn, and Ruthanne arrived to pick up Trixie for a trip to the mall before she could call the police about the notebook and the cave. The trio was late, and the clock hands on Echo's desk seemed to be crawling.

"Where have you guys been?" Echo cried when the two finally arrived. "You were supposed to be here hours ago!" Caught up in her own anxiety, she didn't notice how quietly they entered or how pale and strained their faces were.

"*One* hour ago," Trixie corrected, giving her a suspicious look. "What's the big deal, anyway? I used the time to study for finals. You should have done the same thing, instead of pacing back and forth like a caged tiger. Echo, are you waiting for someone?" Her eyes narrowed. "You didn't invite Pruitt over here, did you?"

"No! I just . . . I have to study for finals, and I need peace and quiet for that."

"Something's happened," Marilyn interrupted quietly, taking a seat on Trixie's desk chair. "Something terrible."

Oh, God, Echo thought. And Trixie said, "No! I don't want to hear this! I don't want to know about it. Let's just go to the mall and go shopping and pretend that everything is just fine. Can we do that, please? Please?"

Deejay shook her head. Wispy dark tendrils clung to the round, smooth cheeks. "Can't, Trixie. There are cops down there, checking every car that leaves campus. We can't pretend *that's* normal."

Trixie sighed heavily, leaned against the closet door. "Okay, then, okay! What *is* it? Is it really bad?"

Ruthanne nodded heavily. There were pain lines around her mouth and, as she spoke, she bent and began rubbing her left leg. "It's horrible. The biker attacked a runner on the river path. Gabriella Stone, the tall, really thin girl on the relay team. Do you know her?"

Trixie and Echo both shook their heads negatively. "Is she okay?" Echo asked, her voice unsteady.

Ruthanne began rubbing the right leg. "No. She's dead. She was crushed against a tree."

Trixie burst into tears, and Echo sagged against the wall. Another one! Another victim had died at the hands of the Mad Biker. And Echo had known the whole time who the guilty party was. If only she hadn't waited for Trixie to leave, if she'd called the police first thing this morning, maybe Gabriella Stone would still be alive.

"That's why we were late," Deejay explained. "When I pulled my car out onto Campus Drive, an ambulance was blocking the way, and traffic was backed up. There were policemen there, and I asked one what had happened. He told us. Didn't want to, I could tell, but I made a pest of myself. Then I turned around and came the back way. Like I said, the cops are checking every car that leaves campus. That's why the traffic was backed up."

Sickened by the news, Echo began shaking from head to toe. She moved backward until her legs bumped against her bed, and then sank down on it. She couldn't think, didn't want to think. Couldn't feel, either. She went completely numb.

No one said anything for a while. Then, "Pruitt's going to be really bummed," Deejay said quietly. "He knew her."

Echo's head snapped up. "Pruitt knew Gabriella Stone?" Like he knew Nancy Becker?

"Yeah. They were on the debating team together first semester. Fighting for the same slot. Gabriella got it, so Pruitt dropped out. He didn't seem at all upset about it. You know Pruitt. He doesn't get wrecked over stuff like that."

That wasn't the Pruitt Echo knew. The Pruitt she knew got very "wrecked" when things didn't go his way.

Marilyn spoke up, her face very white. "Pruitt knew Nancy Becker *and* Gabriella Stone?" she asked Deejay.

"Yeah. Why?"

"Well, don't you think it looks a little like Pruitt is under some kind of curse? Maybe Echo should stay away from him."

Like I have a choice, Echo thought.

"A curse? Marilyn, come off it. Lots of people on campus knew Nancy and Gabriella. They were both popular. I still say Echo is safer with Pruitt around than she is alone. So don't make her afraid of him."

Echo laughed to herself. Too late. But she wasn't afraid of him because of any curse. She was afraid of him because she knew, better than anyone, what he was capable of. Gabriella Stone hadn't known that, or she would have let Pruitt have that slot on the debating team.

Then Deejay astounded Echo by saying, "Trixie, if you're coming with us, you'd better fix your face. Your eyes are a mess."

Echo lifted her head to stare. "You're not still going to the mall, are you? After what's happened?"

Wiping her eyes with a tissue, Trixie stood up and grabbed her purse, saying bitterly, "We'll be a lot safer at the mall than we are here. I think you should come with us, Echo. You look too upset to stay here alone."

But Echo wasn't going anywhere. Gabriella Stone's horrible death could have been prevented. There'd be no trips to the mall or anywhere else until the police had been clued in on the biker's real identity.

As for checking the cars leaving campus, as Deejay said the police were doing, that was a complete waste of time. What were they looking for, anyway? Suppose they *did* stop Pruitt on his way off campus? First of all, he wouldn't be on a motorcycle, he'd be driving his car. And second, you couldn't tell by looking at Pruitt that he was a homicidal maniac. It didn't show.

She felt like screaming when Trixie ran back into the bathroom at the last minute to repair her eye makeup. Would they *ever* leave?

"I really wish you'd stay away from Pruitt, Echo," Marilyn said. The remark caught Echo off guard. She had never witnessed Marilyn defying Deejay or anyone else before. "I mean, I know he's a friend of mine, sort of, but I keep thinking that he knew both those girls and now they're dead."

Before Echo could respond Ruthanne said sharply, "Marilyn, what are you getting at?"

Marilyn's cheeks reddened. "Well, we don't *know* who the Mad Biker is, right? So if we don't know, we can't know it's not Pruitt for sure, can we?"

Ruthanne's jaw dropped, and then her laughter filled the room. When she finally stopped laughing she gasped, "Pruitt? You think Aaron Pruitt is the Mad Biker, Marilyn? Oh, God, Deejay, Echo, have you ever heard anything so ridiculous? I mean, can you *imagine* him even sitting on a motorcycle? The image just does *not* compute, Marilyn. A curse, maybe, but the Mad Biker, Pruitt? Never!"

Watching Ruthanne burst into laughter again, Echo thought despairingly, that's exactly the reaction I'd get from the police if I sent them to Pruitt's room to check him out. One look and they'd hoot with laughter, just like Ruthanne. Unless I had airtight proof.

"Look," Deejay said, "I don't know *who* the Mad Biker is. All I know is, Echo is better off with Pruitt hanging around her than she is all alone.

After all," Deejay continued, "Gabriella Stone might still be alive if she hadn't been running around campus all by herself. Doesn't seem to me that it's a good time for anyone to be alone. Echo has a habit of wandering around campus by herself. At least now she'll be with Pruitt. He's better than nothing."

Wrong, Echo disagreed silently. Pruitt is so much *worse* than nothing!

Trixie emerged finally, and the four left, telling Echo they'd see her later. Unless I'm in jail or dead, Echo thought, both of which are possible. She gave them no more than four seconds before her fingers began jabbing at numbers on the telephone.

"The motorcycle you're looking for in connection with the biker incidents in town and on campus," she said in a strained but audible whisper when someone answered at the police station, "is hidden in one of the caves on the other side of the railroad bridge from campus. The cave closest to the top of the hill, in the middle. You'll find that bike there. There's other stuff, too. Hurry, hurry! Before someone else dies."

Sweating profusely, her hands shaking, Echo replaced the receiver. The voice on the other end was still urging her to stay on the line.

She fell backward onto her bed, lay on her back staring up at the ceiling. She'd done it! She had actually done it. Not in time for Gabriella Stone. But maybe in time to keep someone else alive.

It wouldn't be over when they found the bike, she knew that. The police didn't have the notebook, and they hadn't seen Pruitt's reaction when she'd mentioned the name "Ross" to him. That would all have to wait. Let them find the bike first, and the mini-mechanic's shop established in the cave. They'd check the fingerprints on the bike and, if there weren't any on the bike because he'd been too careful, there would be prints on the tools or the canned goods, on *something* in the cave. Maybe he hadn't had gloves on every time he lifted the face shield, and had left prints on the smoky-colored plastic. They would find prints somewhere in that cave, she was sure of it. Then they'd match the prints to Pruitt's.

Once he'd been taken into custody, only then would she take the notebook to the police station, explain where she'd found it, and let *them* figure out what it all meant. Who *was* Ross, anyway?

With Pruitt in jail, she'd be safe, and so would everyone else.

But not Gabriella Stone. Or the others. It was too late for them.

Echo had intended to wait two hours before calling the police station back to see what they'd found out. But she only lasted an hour and forty-five minutes. Then she dialed.

Without giving her name, and lowering her voice to an unnatural croak, she told the officer who answered that she had called earlier and given an anonymous tip about the bike attacks. "I'm calling to see if the biker has been arrested," she added. "If he has, I have more information for you."

"Yeah, well I have some information for you," the officer said harshly. "The next time you send police out on a wild goose chase, be prepared to spend some time in jail yourself! This whole community is in an uproar over those bike attacks, and we don't have time to be scouring hillsides looking for phantom motorcycles."

Echo was so upset she reverted to her own voice. "You didn't find the cave? I *told* you exactly where it was!"

"Oh, we found it, all right, miss. But it was empty. Clean as a whistle. Nothing there. There *were* tire tracks on the hill, but they were too messed up to do us any good. Besides, they could have been made by anybody doing some off-road riding. Now don't bother us again, okay, or I'll have the call traced and we'll come knocking on your door."

Echo slammed the phone back into its cradle. She couldn't believe it! Pruitt had emptied out the cave this morning? How was that possible?

She'd spooked him, that was obvious. By shredding the tires. Knowing that someone had been in the cave and found the bike had rattled him. So he'd gone back up there . . . when? Last night? This morning? Before or after he'd attacked Gabriella Stone? He'd moved every-thing? *Everything?*

Her expression grim, Echo scooped up the black notebook and left the room.

She went straight to the police station in town.

Chapter 15

Echo was very nervous on the shuttle bus ride to the police station in town. What if Pruitt was watching her? He could have seen her climb on the bus, might even have seen the black notebook in her hand and realized what it was. He'd follow the bus, be waiting for her when she stepped off.

And then what would he do?

The same thing he'd done to Gabriella Stone.

Echo shivered, and slumped deeper into the seat at the very back of the bus. Maybe she wouldn't get off at the police station. Maybe she'd just keep sitting right here and let the bus take her all the way back to campus. Then she'd get off and dump the notebook into the nearest incinerator chute. When she found Pruitt, she'd tell him what she'd done, prove to him that she wasn't going to fink on him. Then he'd get out of her life once and for all.

After all, it wasn't Echo Glenn's job to catch criminals.

But Echo immediately recognized the trouble with her little scenario. Pruitt wasn't going to let her go, just like that, no matter what she did. He *liked* being seen on campus with her, pretending they were dating, and he wasn't about to give that up.

She got off the bus at the police station. Her body was stiff with tension. Her fingers curled tightly around the edges of the black notebook.

The police station was busy. Echo was told to wait. She took a seat on a bench against one wall. Her stomach was churning, her head pounding, and the instinct to run while she still could kept tugging at her legs.

She was still sitting there, stiff and unmoving as a statue, when Liam McCullough walked into the station and took a seat beside her. Her stomach rolled over at the thought of being seen here by someone she knew. Liam knew Pruitt. What if he got to Pruitt before the police did and said, "Hey, Pruitt, guess who I ran into at the police station in town? That girl you're dating, Echo Glenn." Then what?

Then she was dead.

"Hey," Liam said casually. "What's up? What are you doing here?"

She didn't look at him. "Lost my wallet at

the mall. Some kind soul found it and turned it in. I'm here to pick it up." Considering the very real trouble she was already in, a small white lie seemed insignificant. He'd find out the truth about her soon enough. But not yet. Not yet. "What about you?"

"The cops want me to look at some mug shots of area bikers. I told them I didn't see the guy's face the other night at Johnny's Place. He had a helmet on and a face shield. I wouldn't know him if he walked right up to me and said hello. But they want me to look, anyway, so I said okay." He glanced over at Echo. "They're going to throw the book at the guy. And his partner won't get off lightly, either."

Echo raised her head. "His partner?"

"Yeah, you know. The guy who was with him. Or girl. Looked too skinny to me to be a guy. No shoulders. The officer I talked to said he's as guilty as the biker. He should have tried to stop the guy."

"How could anyone tell if he was trying to stop the driver or not?" Echo said a bit defensively. "Maybe he said not to do it and the biker just wouldn't listen. Besides, no one died at Johnny's Place. But two people died when he pushed that car over the cliff, and he was alone then. So I don't think he has a partner."

Liam shrugged. "Doesn't matter. If the cops

can prove there was a second person even one time, that person will hang right along with the biker."

"But that's not fair!" Echo cried. Her voice was shrill with anxiety and several policemen working in the area looked her way. "I mean," she added more quietly, "it doesn't seem fair that someone should be punished for things they weren't involved in."

"Guilt by association. The biker's a maniac. Whoever was with him on that bike at Johnny's Place should have known better." Liam gingerly touched his injured wrist, still in its plaster cast. "Anyway, is it fair that Lily's going to be paralyzed? Is it fair that Polk Malone and Nancy Becker won't live to see twenty-one?" He turned his head again to look at Echo. "Maybe you should save your concern for them instead of worrying about either of those bikers."

What frightened her now was knowing that Liam was only telling her what a police officer had told *him*. If he was quoting accurately, she wasn't going to get any sympathy or understanding here. They were out to get the passenger on that bike in front of Johnny's Place. If she told them what she knew, she wouldn't just be giving them Pruitt. She'd be giving them Echo Glenn, too.

And while they might have a hard time believing that neatnik Pruitt was guilty, they wouldn't have the same problem believing that she was.

She'd been crazy to think she could pull this off. As crazy as Pruitt.

"I just remembered," she said breathlessly, jumping to her feet, "I have a dentist appointment in ten minutes." She put a hand to her jaw. "I've got this tooth, it's been killing me all day. I'll just have to come back here later."

"Do you want me to get your wallet and bring it to campus?" he called after her.

But she was already down the steps and out of the building.

When she was safely back in the dorm, she threw herself down on the bed and began a wrestling match with her conscience. She *had* to turn in Pruitt, before someone else died. It was risky, she knew. If they didn't have enough to hold him and they let him go, he would know who had turned him in. And he'd kill her, just as he'd promised.

She didn't want to die, but she didn't want anyone else to die, either.

She was going to make herself crazy, going over it and over it. Especially when there didn't seem to be any answer.

With shaking fingers, she picked up the

phone and dialed the police station again. This time, she gave the officer who answered Pruitt's name and address. "He's the Mad Biker," she said, and hung up.

She was too tired to do anything, too tired to think. She would just lie here and wait to see what happened.

For the first time in a very long time, Echo wished she had someone to talk to.

Maybe she shouldn't have been so stand-offish with Deejay, Ruthanne, and Marilyn. Even talking to Trixie might be better than wrestling with this horrible, terrifying disaster all by herself.

Well, maybe not. Echo made a face of distaste.

When a knock sounded suddenly on her door, she thought at first that it was the police, coming to tell her they'd arrested Pruitt. Then she realized the police had no reason to come to her room. They didn't *know* she'd made that phone call. She hadn't given her name.

"Echo? Are you in there?"

Liam. That was Liam McCullough's voice. What was *he* doing here?

Echo got up and went to open the door.

"Thought you might like to go for a walk," he greeted her. "I don't like the reason *why* we have the day off, but that shouldn't stop us from

167

taking advantage of it." He smiled down at her. "You look like you could stand to get out of this room."

Pruitt's words of warning rang in Echo's ears. "I have my ways of dealing with competition." She knew she should heed that warning, for Liam's sake. Pruitt was a very dangerous person who didn't make idle threats. He'd already proved that.

"Could we walk down along the riverbank?" she asked. It was behind campus, far from Pruitt's fraternity house. Less chance that he would spot her walking with Liam.

"We can walk anywhere you want. Is that a yes?"

She knew it was risky, but if she stayed alone in her room another second *she'd* go crazy. "That's a yes," she said clearly.

If Liam wondered at the defiance in her voice, he didn't comment on it. "Good. And maybe after our walk, we can go to Vinnie's for pizza. My treat, since you probably don't have your wallet. And how's the tooth?"

Wallet? Tooth? Oh, great, she'd almost forgotten that she'd lied to him about what she was doing at the police station. What a crummy criminal she made! "Oh, the tooth's okay. And I did get my wallet. I went back later, after the dentist. You'd already left. Did you recognize any of the pictures the police showed you?" Of course he hadn't. Pruitt's picture wouldn't be in one of those mug books.

He shook his head. "No. Some really creepy-looking characters in those books, though. But not a single familiar face. I'm grateful. I wouldn't want to think that anyone I knew could have been on that bike at Johnny's Place."

Echo turned away quickly, to keep him from seeing the guilt in her face. *She* had been on that bike, and he knew *her*. What would he say if he found out?

She didn't want to know.

Echo felt that she could really like Liam but a relationship between the two of them could never go anywhere. Never.

But she was past the point of caring. She was going to do this because she wanted to. She needed to be with someone — anyone — other than Aaron Pruitt. And whatever happened, happened.

She wondered as they left the room if Pruitt would call while she was gone, and wonder where she was.

Although a tremor of fear ran along her spine at the thought of how angry he would be when she failed to answer, she also felt a strong surge of satisfaction that, at this moment at least,

Pruitt wasn't pulling her strings.

The satisfaction died a quick death. It was erased by her next thought which was: You will pay dearly for this, Echo Glenn.

She only hoped Liam wouldn't pay, too.

They walked and talked for over an hour, then headed on across the road to Vinnie's where they joined a table that included Deejay and Marilyn, and Liam's best friend, Archie Bordeaux.

Later when Echo went to the restroom with Deejay and Marilyn, Deejay said, "I don't think that Pruitt would be very happy about you being here with Liam, Echo."

Remembering Pruitt's threats, Echo stopped brushing her hair. She said with false bravado, "Pruitt is *not* my keeper. I don't know where you got that idea, Deejay. I've seen one movie with him, that's all."

"Yeah, but I've seen you talking to him on campus. And I know he has a thing for you. I've seen him following you."

Echo's eyes narrowed. "You have? When?"

"All the time. He stays far enough behind so you can't see him, but he's there, all right."

"You should have told Echo," Marilyn said disapprovingly. "That's weird, that he's following her. Pretty creepy, if you ask me."

"I just told her," Deejay said calmly. "I

thought it was kind of nice, myself. I mean, he's obviously watching out for her, making sure the Mad Biker doesn't get her. Don't you think, Echo?"

Hardly. Echo's skin felt clammy. Had Pruitt followed her here tonight? Was there a chance that he might be waiting for her outside the restaurant? That he'd see her come out with Liam, and he'd be furious, knowing she had ignored his warning?

"I'm not sure why he's doing it, Deejay. But I think maybe you're right. He probably wouldn't be at all happy if he knew I was here with Liam. I think I'd better go. Tell Liam I have a headache, okay?"

And although both girls called out a protest, Echo was already out of the restroom and on her way out of the restaurant, leaving by the back entrance so that Liam wouldn't see her go.

Liam would probably be mad. They'd had a good time tonight.

But . . . mad was better than dead.

Pruitt wasn't waiting for her.

As she hurried back to the dorm alone, Echo was sure she could feel eyes on her back. Several times, she whirled around, hoping to surprise him, but she saw nothing.

Back in her room, she was just about to get

ready for bed when there was another knock on the door.

She opened it to find two uniformed police officers standing in the hall.

"Echo Glenn?" one asked. "Are you Echo Glenn?"

She caught her breath and nodded, too shocked to speak. Were they going to arrest her? Oh, God, no.

"We'd like you to come with us, Miss. There's the matter of an anonymous phone call that needs to be cleared up. We were told you could help us."

Echo let out a small sigh of relief. They hadn't come to arrest her. Then what . . . ?

"Who?" she asked. "Who said I could help you?"

The officer glanced down at a small white pad in his hand. "Guy's name is Aaron Pruitt. If you'll just come with us?"

Chapter 16

"Pruitt?" Echo said, swallowing hard.

The officer nodded. "Just trying to clear something up, miss. We received an anonymous telephone call today, accusing Mr. Pruitt of being the biker who's been causing so much trouble around here lately. Mr. Pruitt tells us you made the call."

Well, of course, Pruitt had guessed who made the call. Who else could have made it?

"If you'll just come along with us, to Mr. Pruitt's fraternity house, maybe we can get this all straightened out right now."

"Why didn't he come here?" Echo asked defensively. "Why do I have to go there?"

The officer shifted uncomfortably. "Please just cooperate, Miss Glenn." He glanced at his partner, who seemed to be having trouble hiding a smile. "To tell you the truth, the guy doesn't exactly fit the profile of a biker, if you know what I mean."

"Oh, I know what you mean," Echo said harshly. "But appearances can be deceiving."

"I'll go with you," she told the police officers. "Let Pruitt tell me to my face that I'm a liar."

But Pruitt was too smart for that. He didn't call her any names at all. He took an entirely different tack, his voice smooth as butter. "Tell them the truth now, Echo," he said condescendingly when Echo was standing just inside his door, flanked by the two police officers. "Tell the officers you didn't mean it, that you were just really mad at me and wanted to get me in trouble." To the officers, he said, "Look, what can I say? She's got this thing for me, and she's a pretty girl and all, but I'm not interested. Can't help the way we feel, can we? I've tried to be nice, but she just won't take no for an answer. When she left here this morning after I told her no dice for the twentieth time, she swore she'd get even with me. I guess her phone call to you was an attempt to do just that."

Echo knew how it looked. She saw the officers glancing around the impeccably neat room, saw them studying Pruitt's immaculate appearance. There wasn't a hair out of place on Pruitt's head, not a smudge on his khaki pants, not a wrinkle on him anywhere. While she . . . well, she looked like she hadn't slept in weeks, her hair was helter-skelter all over her head, and she was wearing an old, faded sweatsuit.

"Just in case you need further proof," Pruitt said, bending to remove something from a dresser drawer, "I've been keeping a record of the incidents of harassment. Every time she called or bugged me on campus, I put it in this book. Here, take a look!"

"Let me *see* that!" Echo cried, but the officers were already scanning the pages. When they were satisfied, one reached out to hand it back to Pruitt. Echo intercepted it to do her own scanning.

"This isn't even his handwriting," she announced a moment later. She looked at Pruitt with contempt. "I've seen his handwriting, and this is entirely different. He didn't write this."

"Where have you seen my handwriting?"

Oh, God. She didn't want him to know she had the notebook. "In class," she said staunchly. "You wrote on the blackboard, remember?" That was true, he had, although she hadn't paid the slightest bit of attention to his handwriting then.

"Look, I'll show you," Pruitt said, reaching toward his desk for a piece of paper and a pen.

He scribbled a few words. "There!" he said, extending the piece of paper toward the policemen and Echo. "Doesn't that match the entries in my journal?"

It did. Perfectly. The t's were crossed the same, the i's dotted with little round circles, and the l's looped in exactly the same way.

Echo was dumfounded. "That's not right," she said, shaking her head. "He's tricking you." But she knew how foolish she must sound.

Pruitt shook his head, too, but patiently, tolerantly, as if he were dealing with a stubborn child. "If there's one thing I know about Echo Glenn," he said, "it's that she doesn't give up easily. If she did, we wouldn't be having this situation now, would we?"

"Echo Glenn," the shorter of the two officers mused aloud. "Where have I heard that name before?"

"Well, it's an unusual name," Echo said helplessly, knowing what was coming.

"She's been in trouble on campus a lot," Pruitt offered. "You guys had to be called to campus when she almost started a riot on the steps of the library a while back, verbally attacking the administration. I know you have your job to do," he said sympathetically, "but if I were you, I wouldn't take her word for anything. She's a flake. Ask anyone."

Echo's face burned.

The taller officer turned to her and asked, "Can you prove these allegations against Mr. Pruitt?" he asked. "He says he doesn't own a motorcycle. But you say he does. Where would that motorcycle be?"

"He hides it," she answered, her voice cold. "It was in a cave on the other side of the river, the one in the middle, closest to the top of the hill. But he moved it. I don't know where it is now, but it's around here somewhere. I'm sure you can find it."

"A cave on the hill?" Pruitt said, looking amused. "How original."

"We've looked, miss. No sign of a bike here. No black leather, no boots, no nothing."

She stared at Pruitt. He'd ditched the boots?

He stared right back at her, his eyes slivers of gray ice.

"Ask him about Ross!" she cried, desperate now. She would have to mention the notebook after all. If she only had it. "I found a notebook with these weird things written in it, telling why the biker was hurting people. Pruitt wrote it. And he mentioned someone named Ross. It was because of this Ross person that he was hurting people."

"Where is this notebook now?" Pruitt asked. "I'm sure the police would like to see it. So would I." To the officers, he said calmly, "I don't know anyone named Ross."

Echo's flush deepened. "I . . . I don't have the notebook with me. It's in my room."

Her heart turned over when she saw the skepticism flooding the officers' faces. Pruitt was so convincing. He would simply deny ownership of the notebook, saying that it wasn't his handwriting.

How did he do that? Write in an entirely different hand? He must have been practicing.

"Look, miss," one officer said, "you can understand our position. Mr. Pruitt denies all knowledge of the bike attacks, and there's no proof at all to contradict his denial. I'm afraid our hands are tied."

"But . . ." Echo protested.

"And," the second officer said firmly, "don't be making any more phone calls unless you can back them up, okay? We don't have time right now to be running all over the place following false leads."

Exactly what the desk sergeant had said after she'd made that call about the cave and it had proved to be empty.

There was no point in showing them the notebook now. They'd be positive she'd written the words herself.

The policemen offered to escort her back to

her dorm, but before she could accept their offer, Pruitt stepped forward. "If you don't mind, sergeant," he said, "I'd like to talk with Miss Glenn for a few minutes, see if we can get this straightened out."

"I'm not staying here with him!" Echo cried. "I don't care what you people say, he's dangerous!"

"Let's get something straight," the taller officer told her in a firm, no-nonsense voice. "You've caused a lot of trouble today, making unfounded accusations. If Mr. Pruitt is willing to straighten things out so that something like this doesn't happen again, I'd take him up on it. It's a very generous offer. If I was him, I don't know that I'd be quite so tolerant. If you want, we'll wait right outside. But get this taken care of, okay?"

The offer to remain outside in the hall wasn't meant to protect her, Echo knew that. They didn't see Pruitt as a threat. They just wanted to make sure she stayed there long enough to "straighten things out."

When they had gone, closing the door after them, Pruitt smiled at her. The smile was arrogant, satisfied, with only a hint of anger. "You probably think I'm furious, don't you? Because you finked on me. But actually, you've done me a favor. You were foolish enough to accuse me without proof. Now, they'll never believe anything you say about me again."

Echo knew he was right. Her head began to ache fiercely.

"However," he added, the smile disappearing, the eyes turning icy again, "you *did* betray me, Echo. Your effort may have been futile, but your intent was betrayal. I warned you what would happen if you told."

A wave of dizziness swept over Echo. If she hadn't known the officers were just beyond the door, her knees would have collapsed beneath her.

"But I'm not ready to kill you," Pruitt continued. "I'm not finished with you yet. And," he tapped an index finger lightly against his lips, "I don't know when I will be. It's fun having a pretty girl to show off around campus. And you're no longer any threat to me. Anyway, judging by the look on your face, I'd say being seen around campus with me is a better punishment than killing you." He smiled again. "Am I right?"

"Yes," she snapped, "you're right! I'd rather be dead than seen on campus with you!"

"Well, yes, but you don't have any choice, do you? And I wouldn't be wishing for death so casually if I were you. Someone just might grant your wish."

Echo wished the officers could hear Pruitt threatening her. But the door was closed. "You've killed innocent people," she cried.

"I guess they were just at the wrong place at the wrong time." He shrugged carelessly.

"That's what you said about Lily!" Echo cried. "You drove straight at her! There was no way she could have avoided the bike. You never intended her to, and you know it."

"Maybe I was bored and needed some excitement. Life on campus is really pretty dull, don't you think, Echo?" He moved away from her, to the windowsill, where he reached down and inspected the potted plants. With his back to her, he said, "I'll let you know when I want your company on campus again. It'll be soon, I promise." Then he added, his voice gone cold and harsh, "And stay *away* from Liam McCullough, or you'll *both* be sorry!"

Echo moved to the door and opened it. Deejay had been telling the truth. Pruitt *had* been following her. Otherwise, how would he know about Liam?

Disheartened and thoroughly frightened, Echo let the officers walk her back to Lester. She didn't waste her breath trying to convince them she was telling the truth. What was the point?

It wasn't until she was back in her room that

she guessed the truth about the handwriting. In the journal she'd found in the cave, Pruitt had written about an arm injury. He'd written that he was having trouble writing. No wonder the journal entries had looked a little weird. He'd written them with a seriously injured arm!

Echo reached for the telephone, and then quickly let her hand drop. Suppose she did call the police and explain about the difference in handwriting? Would they listen to her?

Not likely. The officers had made it very clear that they believed Pruitt, not her. There wouldn't be any point in contacting them until she'd found the bike and enough proof to link it positively to Pruitt.

She reached under her pillow for the notebook. She was glad she hadn't shown it to them. It just would have convinced them further that she would do anything to frame Pruitt, because he'd rejected her.

Her fingers slid around under the pillow, expecting to feel the hard cover of the notebook.

They touched nothing but the cool, rumpled sheet.

Echo sat up, and lifted the pillow.

The notebook was gone.

Chapter 17

Echo put her empty hands in her lap. No wonder Pruitt had insisted she show him and the police officers the notebook. He *knew* she didn't have it. He'd slipped into her room somehow and stolen it. He must have seen her with it at some point and realized what it was.

Was he watching her every second of the day?

Sick at heart and feeling trapped, as if she were still in that crevasse in the cave, squeezed between two solid rock walls with no way out, Echo went to bed.

Tuesday morning, she discovered very quickly that Liam *was* mad about her leaving Vinnie's so abruptly. She saw him on campus shortly after her first two classes. When he passed her on the walkway, he refused to speak to her. His face flushed angrily and he brushed by her as if he'd never met her.

Not that she was surprised. He must have been incredibly embarrassed when Deejay and Marilyn came back to the table to announce that Echo had left. Sneaked out the back way, like a common criminal.

Well?

I'm not, she told herself, I'm *not* a criminal.

So why did she feel like one?

She went to the rest of her morning classes, ate lunch alone on the riverbank, attended her afternoon classes, and then walked slowly to the infirmary for her shift, glancing around her continually for some sign of Pruitt.

The first thing she did when she got there was try the medical records file cabinet again.

To her astonishment, the drawer labelled "P-R" opened and slid forward smoothly and quietly.

Someone had forgotten to lock it.

She located Pruitt's file after only a moment, and sagged against the cold metal cabinet in disappointment. There was no "Ross" listed under "Relatives," living *or* dead.

How could that be? She'd been so sure.

Maybe the "Ross" mentioned in the now-missing journal was only a close friend, no relation to Pruitt at all. But then why were his parents so shattered by the death?

She closed the cabinet, more confused than

ever. She had focused on the unidentified Ross, someone she had thought of as Pruitt's close relative, maybe a brother or a cousin, as the motive behind Pruitt's madness. Without Ross, what did she have?

Not much.

A rash of sunburn and insect bite cases from the day off came in then, and Echo was busy for a while. Then there were towels to be washed, dried and folded, and sweeping to do. When the night nurse asked if Echo would stay while she grabbed a quick bite to eat, she said sure. She felt relatively safe in the infirmary, and she wasn't in any hurry to go back to her dorm room.

When she did leave, she regretted that decision. It was already dark. Campus was so quiet. The student body and the faculty had been stunned by the violent deaths of the Miata's occupants and the lone runner. A heavy silence filled with dread seemed to have settled over the rolling lawns and tall stone and brick buildings.

Echo walked with her head down, her shoulders hunched. Realizing that she was hoping Deejay, Marilyn, and Ruthanne would be visiting Trixie when she got back to their room surprised her. But the more, the merrier, seemed like a good idea right about now. The room would feel safer if it was crowded and noisy.

She was just about to step off the curb and cross the Commons when she heard the sound that inevitably sent icy tremors of alarm up her spine. That roar, that low, growling roar spilling out of the darkness from somewhere behind her . . . she knew it could only be one thing.

She whirled around, and tried to race back to the safety of the infirmary, but before her legs would do her mind's bidding, the roar was right there, right at her back. Then strong, viselike hands were around her waist, yanking her backward, pushing her down on the leather seat. Her wrists were pulled forward and pinioned tightly in front of the black leather jacket as the bike, its light on now, roared off into the darkness.

It had all happened so quickly, Echo hadn't had time to catch her breath to make a sound. Hadn't screamed, hadn't shouted, hadn't called out for help. She had kicked and slapped, but to no avail.

Now, she screamed. But the rushing wind swallowed up her cries.

And then they were racing along the highway toward town. He drove with one hand, using the other to keep her wrists imprisoned around his waist. The grip forced her to lean so far forward, her face was roughly pressed against the back of his jacket.

"Where are we going?" she shouted into the smooth black leather. "Where are you taking me?"

No answer. Only the steady slap-slap of the wind against her cheek.

He was angry because she'd been with Liam the night before? This was her punishment?

Where were they going?

The bike raced on through the cool, dark night. Trees and houses and cars whizzed by in a dizzying blur. Echo's eyes began to tear. From the wind, she told herself, although she couldn't be sure they weren't tears of fright.

They didn't go all the way into town. Instead, when they neared a minimart just outside of town, the motorcycle suddenly veered sharply to the right and crossed the highway, racing into the parking lot and narrowly missing one of two yellow gas pumps.

Only then did he let go of Echo's hands, to maneuver the bike. But her sudden sense of freedom was short-lived, because the biker never slowed down enough for her to jump clear.

The bike slammed, full force, into a parked, compact car, denting a fender. Echo's body lifted up off the seat and she might have been flung off if he hadn't reached behind him with one hand to slam her back into place. The bike bounced backward, veered around the car, and then raced forward to target a tall stack of tires.

Echo screamed as the tower toppled sideways. Tires, looking like giant doughnuts, rolled out across the parking lot, some bumping up against the gas pumps, others escaping onto the highway.

And still the bike failed to slow down. Its speed, plus the certainty that if she jumped free Pruitt would run over her as he had Lily, kept Echo frozen in place.

The motorcycle raced backward, whirled around, and sped toward the entrance to the small store just as a woman in a long, brown coat carrying two sacks of groceries, opened the door and stepped out.

"Don't hit her!" Echo screamed. "Don't hit that woman!"

But Pruitt bore down and slammed into the defenseless woman.

The woman screamed just once as she was struck and catapulted backward. Cans and boxes of food flew into the air. The victim landed on her back a few feet away, her head slapping against a tall stack of newspapers, which Echo was certain had saved the woman's life. If her head had hit the cement instead, she probably would have been killed instantly.

"Stop it!" Echo screamed, pounding and clawing at the back of the leather jacket. When that didn't work, her fists began hammering against the hard plastic helmet. "Stop it, stop it! Let me get off! Stop!"

The distant sound of a siren reached her ears then. It must have reached Pruitt's, too, because without pausing for even an instant, he raced the bike across the parking lot and out onto the highway, aiming it toward campus.

Echo, her wrists imprisoned again, began crying tears of frustration, fear, and disappointment. If that siren meant that the police were on their way to the minimart, they would arrive too late to apprehend the biker.

The motorcycle made it back to campus in record time. When it pulled up in front of Lester, it failed to come to a complete stop. It slowed a little, but was still very much in motion when Pruitt reached back and gave Echo a brutal shove that sent her off the bike and to the pavement in a heap.

Then he raced away.

Stunned, she lay there for several minutes. She was grateful that there was no one around to witness her humiliation. Or to connect her to the biker. Especially after what had just happened. News of this latest attack would be all over campus by morning.

Her knees, and the palms of her hands were badly scraped and bleeding. But she hadn't hit her head when she tumbled off the bike, and she had no broken bones.

She got to her feet slowly, feeling as if she'd just taken a wild ride on a roller coaster. That poor woman . . . how seriously had she been hurt? Had the owner of the market, who must have been watching from inside, managed to copy down the bike's license number? Even if he had, that wouldn't really help. Pruitt had said the bike wasn't his, that he'd stolen it. And no one but her knew that he had it.

She took a careful step, wincing as the scrapes on her knee stung, then another step and another. She found that although her legs threatened to betray her at any moment and send her crashing to the ground again, she *could* walk. If she could just make it back to her room, she'd be okay.

Now, she hoped desperately that Trixie and her friends would *not* be in the room. No one could see her like this. If they did, when they heard the news about the minimart, they might start wondering.

She got lucky. No one was in the room when

she cautiously opened the door and called Trixie's name. It was empty.

Closing and locking the door with shaking fingers, Echo hurried to her bed and threw herself across it, wincing as her scraped knees and arms came in contact with the scratchy bedspread. After a while, she got up and went into the bathroom, where she cleaned up the scrapes and changed into a green sweatsuit. Her ripped jeans and sweatshirt, both boasting fresh bloodstains, were shoved into a far corner of the closet. She didn't want Trixie asking her about them.

Then she returned to her bed, where she lay for a long time, trembling, too shaken to think.

Chapter 18

The next few days were nightmarish. Pruitt stepped up his demands for Echo's time, and dragged her to a party at the frat house, a play given by the drama department, and a tennis match. Each time he called or came to her room to get her, she swore to herself she wouldn't go. She'd make up some excuse.

And each time, he smiled and whispered, "Tired of living, Echo?" and she remembered Gabriella Stone and Nancy Becker, and she went with him.

She seemed to see Liam McCullough everywhere. He never acknowledged her presence.

"You hurt his feelings," Marilyn said. She, Ruthanne, and Deejay were sitting with Echo and Pruitt at the tennis match. Pruitt had gone to get drinks. "Liam probably can't figure out why you picked Pruitt over him." She shook her head. "I still can't believe you two are an item. No one can."

"Don't be ridiculous, Marilyn," Deejay said. "Echo doesn't have a thing for Pruitt. She's not in love with him, are you, Echo?"

"Go ahead, tell them," Pruitt's voice said as he arrived, drinks in hand. "I don't mind. I want the whole campus to know." He sat down beside Echo, handed drinks all around and wrapped an arm around her shoulders, pulling her close to him. "We can tell our friends how we feel about each other. I don't mind talking about feelings. Go ahead!"

Echo seethed.

Deejay, Marilyn, and Ruthanne stared.

It was one thing, Echo realized, for her to spend time with Pruitt. After all, he was friends with them, too. Sometimes they went places with him. But it was something else entirely to think of someone being *in love* with Aaron Pruitt. They couldn't quite grasp the concept.

If she denied it, he would be livid. He wouldn't kill her . . . he was having too much fun . . . but she was afraid it would send him off on another insane bike attack, taking his anger out on innocent people.

She shrugged. And although she cringed at

the sound of the words as they left her mouth, she said, "Pruitt and I have a lot in common."

Liam McCullough was sitting five rows above them in the bleachers. Echo could feel his eyes on her back.

"Wow," Marilyn breathed, "you and Pruitt. Who'd have thought it?"

"Not me," Deejay said, her eyes returning to the tennis court, and Ruthanne said philosophically, "Well, who can explain love?"

Echo wanted to scream, "It's not love, it's not! It's hate!" Not to mention fear.

In spite of all the time she was spending with Pruitt, Echo had learned nothing useful. Whenever she brought up the motorcycle, Pruitt said, "I am *not* going to tell you where it's hidden, so forget it. We're not going to talk about it."

She was getting nowhere. Meantime, everyone on campus thought she had a thing for Aaron Pruitt. Gag.

Each night when she went to bed, she expected at any moment to hear a knock on the door. She would get up, answer it, and find policemen there, extending a pair of metal handcuffs toward her. "Come along now, miss," they would say. "We don't want any trouble. The owner of the minimart has identified you as the girl on the back of the bike."

And if a knock came and it wasn't the police, it would be Pruitt, come to finish her off for good.

By the end of that week, Echo wanted nothing more than she wanted an end to all of this, one way or the other. She couldn't stand it any more, the fear, the anxiety of waiting for the next biker attack, the confusion about what to do. Pruitt hadn't threatened her lately, but that was because she went with him when he insisted.

She had to find a way out of this.

Make up your mind to do something, Echo, she scolded herself on Thursday night when she was lying in her bed. Make up your mind and then *do* it. Just *do* it!

A knock did come then, but Echo knew immediately that it was neither the police nor Pruitt because Trixie's high, shrill voice called, "Echo! Forgot my key! What'd you lock the door for, anyway?"

Echo let her in.

"I guess it's not such a bad idea, locking the door," Trixie admitted, flopping down on her bed. "Did you hear the latest bit about that minimart attack?"

A silent nod was the only answer she got.

"They said there was a girl with him this time. She wasn't wearing a helmet, and the store owner said her hair was . . ." Trixie tilted her head, stared at Echo. "Was copper-colored. And long. And curly. He said she was fat."

"Who?"

"The girl on the bike," Trixie answered impatiently. "Aren't you listening, Echo? The girl riding with the biker had hair the color of yours, according to the guy on the radio in Tony's car, but she was fat. 'Generously-sized,' he said." Trixie laughed. "Anyway," she got up and moved to the bathroom, "I guess that lets you off the hook. You are most certainly not 'generously-sized,' Echo."

Echo realized then what the store owner must have seen when he heard the commotion outside and hurried to the windowed door. He'd seen her sweatshirt. The thing was so bulky and oversized to begin with. With the bike racing around the parking lot at high speeds, the wind had filled up her sweatshirt with air, like a balloon. When it billowed out around her, she must have looked twenty or thirty pounds heavier than she actually was.

When the phone rang, she answered it, sure that it was for Trixie. But it wasn't.

It was Pruitt.

"Tomorrow night," he said without a greeting. "Movie. At the mall. Pick you up at eight."

"No." Echo kept her voice low, to keep

Trixie, still in the bathroom, from hearing. "I'm not going."

There was a brief silence. And then, "Oh, yeah, you are."

The easy confidence in his voice maddened her. She was *so* sick of that voice! Sick of *him*. "You're a killer, Pruitt," she hissed into the phone. "You kidnapped me and dragged me off to that minimart. And then you blackmailed me into hanging out with you on campus as if we were friends. We're *not* friends, Pruitt!"

"Yeah, right. Tell it to the cops, Echo. I'm sure they'd believe you."

She had never hated anyone so much. "I'm going to find that bike," she said quietly, evenly. "And when I do, the police will link it to you. I will be so thrilled to testify against you, I won't even care if I'm expelled from school."

There was a long silence on the other end of the line.

Trixie opened the bathroom door, a white towel wrapped around her head.

"You're not going to live long enough to find *anything*," Pruitt hissed into the phone. "You never learn, do you, Echo? You *called* the police. You sent them to that cave, and then you sent them to me, and how much good did it do you? Do you really think a single police officer will listen to you now? Go ahead, go hunting in every cave on that hill if you want. But in the meantime, you're going to be keeping me company, you got that?"

She slammed the phone into the cradle, wishing fervently that the noise would shatter Pruitt's eardrum.

"Wow, who was that? You just turned cranberry red."

"No one." True. No one at all.

When Trixie had dried her hair and gone to bed, Echo got up and sat on the windowseat. If you were Pruitt, she asked herself, where would *you* hide the motorcycle that could connect you to several deaths?

The answer came, sharp and clear, as if she were reading a newspaper headline. CLEVER KILLER HIDES MOTORCYCLE IN CAVE ALREADY SEARCHED BY POLICE.

Of course! Could there be a safer place?

Her heart was pounding. If she was right . . . if she found the bike . . . it would be all over, one way or the other. Okay, she'd get in serious trouble, herself. But it would be worth it to get Pruitt off campus forever. So he couldn't hurt anyone ever again.

She didn't have a flashlight. Hers was still somewhere out there on the hill. She wouldn't be surprised if Pruitt had taken it when he cleaned out the cave.

Fumbling around in Trixie's desk drawers, Echo finally found a flashlight. It was pitifully small. She checked to make sure it was working. It was, although the beam was pathetically narrow, and very pale.

It would have to do. If she waited until morning, she'd jump right out of her skin. Sleeping would be impossible.

Almost as an afterthought, she grabbed a nail file off her night table. It was metal, and long, and sharp. Might not scare anyone, but it was better than nothing.

Pocketing the flashlight and yanking a sweater off a closet hanger, Echo left the room, closed the door behind her, and headed down the dim, quiet hall to the elevator.

Chapter 19

Echo couldn't be sure Pruitt wasn't following her as she hurried across a cool, foggy campus, but it didn't seem likely. If he'd been watching their dorm windows from outside, he'd have seen the lights go off. Thinking they'd gone to bed, wouldn't he then have returned to the frat house to sleep? It was very late, almost two in the morning. But then, maybe Pruitt stayed up all night, like bats and vampires and werewolves and other blood-sucking creatures of prey.

At the last minute, Echo changed her plans. Something about Pruitt's medical file had been bothering her. She couldn't put her finger on what it was, she only knew something hadn't seemed right. As she came near the entrance of the infirmary, sitting dark and silent in the foggy mist, she decided to detour before going to the cave. There were no patients in there now, she knew that. The lone doctor on call would be asleep on a cot in the back room. This could be the perfect opportunity to go over Pruitt's file again.

Inside, Echo was grateful that the flash-light's beam was so narrow and pale. Harder for someone to spot her that way. And she knew her way around the infirmary so well, she really didn't need much light.

The medical records file was locked. But breaking into a file cabinet seemed trivial compared to being linked with the Mad Biker. One crime leads to another, Echo thought, and felt in her pockets for the nail file she'd brought.

She used it to pry open the cabinet. It took a while, because she had no idea what she was doing, and every little sound she made brought a scream of protest from her nerves. At one point, she tugged so hard on the drawer handle, a pile of folders waiting to be filed in the draw-ers sailed into the air, landing on the cold white tiles.

When the drawer finally slid open, Echo re-membered what it was that had been bothering her about Pruitt's medical file. Under, "Scars, Birthmarks, Etc., he had written "None." Yet the journal entry had stated quite clearly, "*I will have scars inside and out that will never go away.*"

She *knew* where Pruitt's inside scars were
. . . in his sick and twisted mind. But where
were the visible scars from the motorcycle accident? She had never noticed any.

Fingers fumbling nervously, she checked his
file again. There it was, "Scars — none." And
no mention of "Ross," either.

Echo sat back on her heels, the folder in her
hands. She glanced down at it again, checking
the item labelled "Serious injuries." If you'd
ever had one, you were supposed to check the
box and write in the space allotted what that
injury had been. In the allotted space on
Pruitt's file, there, again, was the word "none."

Had he just not wanted to mention the motorcycle accident that had killed Ross?

Echo replaced the file and closed the drawer,
painfully aware that anyone who took a good
look at the lock would see that it had been
tampered with. But no one would know she had
done it, unless Pruitt was dogging her footsteps even this late at night.

Using her flashlight to guide her, she began
scooping up the spilled folders. She didn't intend to take the time to return each to its cor-
rect place. She shoved all the manila folders
into a pile and would have returned them then
to the top of the cabinet if she hadn't noticed
a name that stopped her.

SEXTON, MARILYN.

Echo felt a pang of sympathy. Marilyn had been in today to see the doctor? Marilyn never complained much, but everyone knew her arms and legs, which had had so much reconstructive surgery after the fire, sometimes plagued her. The whirlpool wasn't always enough. This must be one of those times.

What was it like to be only eighteen and live with so much pain, like Deejay and Marilyn and Ruthanne?

Echo would never have looked inside Marilyn's file, had it been closed. She considered the file private property. She had invaded Pruitt's only because she was desperate for answers.

But Marilyn's file wasn't closed. The primary information sheet was sitting on top of the folder bearing her name. One particular piece of information leaped out at Echo as if to say, "Look! Look at this!"

It was a name written in the list of relatives. The name caught Echo's eye and stilled her hand in the act of replacing the folders.

The name was "Ross."

Marilyn had a relative named Ross?

Had had, Echo realized, her eyes skimming the information. Past tense. Because the name was in the column marked "Deceased." Dead. Gone. No longer alive.

Marilyn's relative named "Ross" was dead.

Cause of death: "Accidental." Marilyn Sexton's relative named Ross had died in an accident.

A motorcycle accident?

Her eyes continued to fly across the paper. She found something else. Marilyn's parents, according to the information she had provided to the university, were still very much alive. Also a brother and two sisters. Hadn't anyone *died* in that awful house fire that had scarred Marilyn so severely?

"I will have scars inside and out that will never go away."

Marilyn Sexton had scars. Lots of them.

Maybe there had never *been* a house fire. Maybe that was why Marilyn never talked about it. Because Marilyn's scars had, instead, been caused by a tragic motorcycle accident that had taken the life of a beloved relative. A brother, maybe.

Such an accident could make someone very, very angry.

Echo looked again, this time to see who "Ross" had been to Marilyn . . . a brother? An uncle?

She blinked when she saw the answer. "Aunt."

Aunt Ross? Ross was a guy's name, wasn't it?

Could be a family name. Echo knew girls named Morgan and Lee. And look who's talking, anyway, she thought, what about your own name?

She replaced the pile of papers on the top of the cabinet, and left the infirmary, lost in thought.

Marilyn? *Marilyn?*

How was Marilyn connected to Pruitt? To the motorcycle? Marilyn couldn't possibly hop on a motorcycle. She had days when she walked almost as stiffly as Ruthanne.

Still . . . if you were as determined as the person who had written that journal, maybe you could do anything if you set your mind to it.

Marilyn?

If she hadn't been so lost in thought, she would have heard the rustling sound coming from the bushes just outside the infirmary, seen the dark figure step out from behind them and then move toward the telephone hanging on the outside of the building.

But Echo was too distracted to notice.

Chapter 20

The closer Echo got to the river, the thicker the fog became. The pale beam of her small flashlight nearly disappeared in the damp, gray mist.

But she kept going. She was more confused than ever now, and she was counting on the cave to give her some answers. *If* she was right about Pruitt being clever enough to return the bike to its original hiding place.

As she hurried, Echo fought to sort out what she'd learned about Marilyn. Marilyn had an aunt named "Ross" who had died an accidental death. Marilyn had visible scars. And no one in Marilyn's family had died in a tragic house fire. Maybe Marilyn and her aunt had been in a motorcycle crash. The aunt had died, all because of a clerk's negligence and cowardice. And Marilyn had vowed revenge, which was why she had never told the truth about the accident. She didn't want anyone connecting her with a motorcycle.

Marilyn?

Then what about Pruitt? Where did he fit in?

It was Pruitt on that bike, Echo was positive. At least . . .

At least, it was Pruitt the first time, when they turned left at Campus Drive and drove along the highway. She had made that appointment with him in person.

But after that . . .

In the leather jacket, the helmet, the face shield, the voice muffled by the roar of the engine, *anyone* could have been driving the bike after that first time. Anyone!

Echo slowed her steps. Was it possible? Could someone have pretended to be Pruitt? Why?

Marilyn knew Pruitt.

I wouldn't have recognized her voice, Echo thought, not over the roar of the bike. Anyone could have been talking to me, anyone at all.

But Pruitt had *admitted* he was the Mad Biker. Had threatened her, scared her half out of her wits because of it.

Echo's heart beat faster as she stumbled through the chill, gray fog. Could Marilyn and Pruitt be working together? Was the Mad

Biker actually *two* people? Marilyn, with her scarred, stiff, arms and legs, couldn't maneuver that bike in a million years. But Pruitt could. He had no scars, no pain.

A twig snapped somewhere behind Echo.

Her heart stopped. Her head swivelled around. She swept the flashlight in an arc, exploring the misty darkness behind her.

Nothing. She saw nothing but fog, wrapping itself around her like a wet wool blanket.

She turned and stepped onto the bridge, hurried across it. It creaked and groaned ominously, as it always did. But she made it across, once narrowly escaping a sudden tumble through a good-sized hole that hadn't been there when she came across the last time.

Tired of wrestling with her new, bizarre information, Echo concentrated on the cave instead. What if she was wrong? What if the cave was still empty, the way the police had found it? Was being out here alone, in the blackness of night, in the wet, clammy fog, her flashlight of very little use, as she slipped and stumbled up this stupid hill, just a waste of time?

Before Echo even entered the cave, she knew no one was in it. She sensed it, could feel it in her bones.

She was right. Inside the cave, she swept the light from side to side.

The bike was there, leaning against one wall.

The tools were there, the changes of clothing, two stacks of books, a few cans of food, and three or four extra tires laying beside the bike.

Echo exhaled deeply. Now what? Here it was, right in front of her. But she wasn't quite sure what to do with it.

She knew this much, though. This time, she had to do it right. No leaving the bike, or any other evidence that she found linking Pruitt to the biking episodes, here in the cave. It came with her when she left. She had no idea how she would manage that. She only knew that it was essential.

Painfully aware of time rushing by, and afraid the fog would thicken into an impenetrable soup, keeping her prisoner on this side of the bridge, Echo began hurriedly searching the cave. She wasn't sure what she was looking for. Something to link Pruitt to the bike. He was the one who had ridden it. He had to be. She'd worry about Marilyn later.

She found the first helpful thing on the floor of the cave, without much searching at all. Books, three of them, with Aaron Pruitt's name on the frontispieces.

But he could always say she'd stolen the

books from his room or some such nonsense. She needed more.

She found it. A driver's license was hidden in the middle of one of the books. It was a motorcycle license, with Pruitt's picture staring up at her. It struck her as she picked it up and fingered it that it hadn't been very well hidden.

But then, Pruitt had been so arrogant about the police never coming into this place again, she was surprised anything was hidden at all.

Were the books and the motorcycle license enough?

Chilled clear through and jumping with nervousness each time she heard a sound outside, Echo kept searching.

Then she found the most valuable piece of evidence hidden in the crevasse where she had sought refuge from Pruitt that first night. It was wrapped in plastic to keep it safe from the steady overhead drip-drip of water.

It was an audio tape labelled, DIARY OF REVENGE.

Echo couldn't believe her luck. There was no time to listen to the tape now, but unless she was seriously mistaken, it was Pruitt recording his marauding adventures on the motorcycle. A death-by-death description, no doubt. For Marilyn, waiting in her room, so that she would be in on every gory detail? Or to satisfy Pruitt's own monumental ego?

She wondered if her name was mentioned on the tape. Probably. But she'd already faced up to the fact that she wasn't going to get out of this mess without consequences. It didn't seem to matter now.

He just couldn't stand not bragging about it, she thought, pocketing the tape. And the chances were excellent that he hadn't bothered to disguise his voice on the tape. Even if he had, a voice analysis machine would take care of that.

Echo turned to stare at the bike. It looked ten times larger and heavier than it ever had before.

I cannot ride that, she thought, feeling sick. It weighs a ton. Even if I could get it started, I'd never be able to steer it. I'll never be able to get it over that bridge. Probably drive it right off the bridge into that deep, cold water.

She knew she had no choice. How else was she going to get the bike to the police? She wasn't leaving it here a second time. This time, it was coming with her.

Keys, keys, she needed the keys to the bike. She would take it and the books and the tape and go straight to the police station. And pray like mad that she didn't run into anyone along the way. Anyone . . . meaning Pruitt.

The keys were hanging from the handlebars, along with the helmet.

Afraid that her hair would mix in with any hairs from Pruitt's head and destroy evidence, Echo left the helmet hanging where it was. If I drive off the bridge, she thought, climbing on the bike's black leather seat, that helmet won't do me any good, anyway.

Dumping the three books with Pruitt's name in them in the rear basket, and pocketing the driver's license, Echo placed the key in the ignition and turned it.

Nothing happened.

She tried repeatedly to start the bike. Turned the ignition key. Jumped on the pedal the way she'd seen Pruitt do, turned the handlebars, copying him.

Nothing.

Nothing happened, not even a chug or a gurgle.

She tried again and again, but she couldn't start the bike.

Nearing tears, she gave up, deciding she had no choice. She would have to push the bike back to campus. She was going to get it back to campus if it killed her.

She pushed up the kick stand and grabbed

the handlebars and push-pulled the heavy bike out of the cave into the fog.

She could see almost nothing.

She couldn't hold the flashlight in her hand and grip the handlebars at the same time, and she didn't know how to turn on the bike's light without power from the engine.

The only thing she had going for her was that she knew the terrain of the hill pretty well by now and knew which spots to avoid.

If she couldn't make it all the way back to campus with the bike, she could at least hide it somewhere else, somewhere Pruitt wouldn't think of looking, until she could browbeat the police into taking a look at it.

Breathing hard, sweating profusely, the muscles in the back of her neck and her shoulders screaming in anger, Echo slowly, slowly, made her way down the hill.

She was almost to the bridge when she heard something.

She stopped. The bike wanted to keep going and tugged violently at her hands until she thought her arms were going to pull out of their sockets, but she held it back.

"What was that?" she whispered, peering into the fog-smoked darkness.

When she first saw the figure, hurrying toward her from the other end of the bridge, she told herself it wasn't real. It didn't *look* real. It looked, in the swirling mist, more like a ghost, amorphous, with no solid limbs or torso.

But it was real, Echo realized as it approached the middle of the bridge. The figure was tall and thin and she could hear, faintly, the sharp hammering of heels on the wooden floor of the bridge. High heels? No. The figure was masculine. Not high heels, boots. The heels of boots on the wooden bridge, that was the sound she heard.

Pruitt.

He hadn't ditched the boots, after all. He'd only hidden them.

Although she knew he couldn't possibly see her yet, he was headed straight toward her. Toward the cave. Coming to check on his bike?

Echo glanced frantically toward her left. Nothing there but dirt and grass. Her head flew to the right. Bushes. Short, stubby, thick, at the end of the bridge. But dangerously close to the edge of the riverbank.

The boot heels pounded closer. Any second now, Pruitt would appear out of the fog and see her standing there with his beloved bike.

The bushes would provide some protection. If the bike didn't slip and go crashing over the edge of the riverbank.

There was no time to think about it, no time to analyze. There was only time to jump behind the bushes and tug the bike in after her. It slid into the bushes and fell heavily on her left ankle. She had to slap a hand over her mouth to keep from screaming in pain.

If she could just stay hidden until he'd crossed the bridge and climbed the hill, that would give her time to grab the bike and race across to campus. *If* he didn't see her when he stepped off the bridge.

But he didn't step off the bridge.

Echo lay behind the bush on the damp ground, hardly breathing, shaking and shivering, her ankle throbbing, so lost in terror that it was several minutes before she realized that the sound of the footsteps had ceased.

Pruitt had stopped. He was no longer advancing across the bridge.

Where *was* he?

Cautiously, carefully, Echo pulled herself to a sitting position and peeked through the branches of the bush. She could see nothing. The fog was too thick, the night too dark, the middle of the bridge too far away.

She straightened up further, kneeling, craning her neck to see. Poked her head out dangerously far, in an effort to discover what was happening. She had to know where Pruitt was.

Then, as if it were anxious to do her bidding, the fog cleared for a moment, and she saw him. Standing in the middle of the bridge, facing away from the water, leaning against the railing. As if . . . as if he were waiting for her. Waiting for *someone*, anyway.

Then she saw the second figure, approaching Pruitt from his end of the bridge. He hadn't been waiting for her, after all, but someone else . . .

Who?

The second figure was feminine. Echo could tell that much by the way it walked.

Marilyn?

Marilyn! Echo thought, sinking back down on her heels. Oh, God, now she had the two of them to contend with. Even if Pruitt continued across the bridge and went on up the hill, Marilyn wouldn't. The climb would be too much for her. She'd wait at the foot of the bridge.

Right . . . beside . . . Echo's . . . hiding place!

Echo straightened up again. As she did, the second figure moved slightly, closer to Pruitt. But it moved too smoothly, too easily, to be Marilyn. Marilyn Sexton had never moved that fluidly in all the time Echo had known her.

Then the figure raised its right arm, in a familiar gesture. It was holding something . . . a stick? A baseball bat? Yes, a baseball bat, held high on one shoulder in what looked like a threat.

One person Echo knew on campus had made a practice of demonstrating different tennis swings to the girls in the whirlpool room. A former championship player undone by a severe case of tennis elbow, Delores Jean Cutter took pride in showing off the form that had won her many awards in the past. At least, she had on those days when her arm wasn't stiff and painful. She was particularly adept at a powerful backhand swing.

And it looked to Echo, watching from her bushes, like a backhand swing with a baseball bat was about to be delivered to Pruitt.

Echo would have known that stance anywhere.

The figure was the right height and weight.

Not the right height and weight for Marilyn Sexton. The right height and weight for former tennis player Delores Jean Cutter.

Deejay.

Deejay turned suddenly, facing Echo's end of the bridge, and began to shout.

"I know you're there, Echo!" Deejay yelled. "I've been watching you. You're in the bushes at the end of the bridge, and you've got the bike. Bring it here. It's mine, and I want it."

Echo stayed where she was.

"Echo!" Louder this time. Angry. "Pruitt here has about two more minutes to live. Don't you want to save your boyfriend?"

Boyfriend?

"He's a dead man, Echo! And if you're not here within thirty seconds, you're dead, too."

Echo stood up. Picked up the bike. Hauled it out of the bushes. Stood at the far end of the bridge, holding onto the handlebars.

Deejay waved an arm, signalling to her to keep coming.

Echo sat on the seat. Turned the key.

And this time the engine roared to life.

She squeezed the accelerator on the handlebars.

The bike took off, flying across the bridge straight toward the pair standing in the middle.

Chapter 21

When she jumped astride the bike, Echo had no plan. She couldn't make a plan when she had no idea what was going on. All she wanted to do was get across the bridge, away from Deejay and Pruitt and whatever new horrors they were up to.

She clutched the handlebars, kept her foot pressed down on the bike's pedal and fought to steer the monstrous machine away from the metal railing on both sides of the bridge.

She might have made it if Deejay hadn't been armed with a baseball bat.

Deejay's timing was perfect. She waited patiently, bat poised in the air, while a white-faced Pruitt cowered against the railing.

When Echo, valiantly trying to steer the bike around the two, was less than a foot away, Deejay swung, using her famous backhand.

The bat caught Echo just beneath the ribs.

The blow lifted her up off the bike and out into the fog. Had she landed on the metal part of the bridge, she would have been knocked unconscious. Instead, she dropped with a thud to the wooden walkway, and although it groaned a protest at the impact of her weight, it softened her landing.

The bike kept going, skidding crazily out of control until it slammed into the railing, bounced off, and came to a rest, its motor dying, not far from Deejay's booted feet.

It was those feet that Echo first saw when she realized she was still alive, still conscious, and that she hadn't been tossed into the river.

At first, she thought the boots were Pruitt's. Snakeskin, with diamonds of wine and green weaving their way up the sides.

Then one of the boots stomped down on Echo's left hand, pinning it to the walkway.

The boots belonged to Delores Jean Cutter.

Too stunned to move, too numb to think, Echo lay on the damp wood, not even feeling the pain in the pinioned hand or in her ribs where the bat had struck.

The boot raised, freeing her hand. Two boots clomped over to the motorcycle. It was lying on its side, at Echo's eye-level. She saw hands reach down, lift it, sensed that Deejay was climbing aboard. But the engine didn't roar to life.

"Pruitt is going to die now," Deejay said, "and you're going to watch, Echo. I'll take care of you permanently when I'm through with him. I've already told him who I am. He knows now, although I have to say it took him by surprise."

"You said your last name was Cutter," Pruitt said sullenly. "Not Costello. How was I supposed to know you were Ross Costello's sister? You never came to court, so I didn't know what you looked like."

Echo lifted her head to look up at him. Ross Costello's sister? Deejay? Deejay had lied about her last name? And she had a brother named Ross? Correction. *Had* had. Ross was dead, that much Echo knew from the journal.

"I never came to court," Deejay said curtly, "because I was lying in a hospital bed. And I didn't want you to know who I was. That would have ruined everything." She glared at Echo. "But Echo did that for me, anyway, didn't you, Echo? She ruined my whole, lovely plan."

With great effort, Echo sat up, slid backward on the wet floorboards until her back was resting against the railing. She could see Pruitt standing with his back against the railing, could feel the metal bars shaking with his trembling. And she could see Deejay, sitting on the bike now, facing him.

"I don't know what's going on," Echo said numbly. "I don't know what you're talking about."

Deejay laughed harshly. "Yes, you do! You read my journal. You know all about it."

"Your journal? That was *your* journal?"

"You weren't supposed to find that. I should have hidden it better. Careless of me, leaving it out like that. You were supposed to think that everything in that cave belonged to Pruitt, and then I went and left my journal lying around. I had to steal it back from you because I was afraid you'd realize that the handwriting wasn't his."

"Deejay, I don't get it. What was I supposed to do?" Echo shook her head to clear her mind.

"You were *supposed* to turn this weasel in to the police! I *gave* you everything you needed! I bought these stupid boots, exactly like his, I took you with me to Johnny's Place so you'd be an eyewitness, and when those things didn't work because you're too stupid to live, I hauled you off to the minimart. I thought the whole time that any minute he'd be arrested because there was an eyewitness, and then you *fell* for him, Echo!" Her voice rose.

"This creep, this cretin, this *murderer*! You fell for him!"

"Oh, God, I did not!" Echo cried. "I *hate* him! I wanted to turn him in, Deejay. I tried. But the cops believed him, not me. And he said he could kill me at any time. I knew he meant it, Deejay. After all the things he'd done, I knew he meant it."

"Oh, you stupid girl!" Deejay moved the bike a foot closer to Pruitt. The railing shook harder. "*He* didn't do anything! I am the biker. I made all the attacks. All of them. To frame *him*. And you were supposed to be my ace in the hole. I'd been following him every chance I got since I first came to Salem. So I saw you talking to him in the library, saw you point to his boots, and knew you thought he was the Mad Biker. Exactly what I wanted, although I wanted the person who noticed the boots to be someone more reliable than you. Someone with a better reputation on campus. I could have waited until someone better noticed the boots, but the school year is almost up and I was afraid to waste any more time. So I had to settle for you. My mistake."

After a moment, she added, "You really weren't in love with him? He was blackmailing you?" Deejay shook her head. "My mistake again. I guess I should have known. Sorry,

Echo. But it's too late now. We'll just have to see this new scenario all the way to the end. I can't change my plans again."

Her statements refused to register in Echo's spinning mind. "No," she said, shaking her head. "It was *Pruitt* on that bike, I know it was." The hand bruised from Deejay's boot pointed at Pruitt. "I *talked* to him. That first night. He *is* the Mad Biker. He never denied it. And he said he would kill me if I didn't do what he said."

Pruitt spoke, then, his voice so unsteady it was almost a falsetto. "I borrowed that bike. The first night."

"You mean you stole it," Deejay corrected, her voice cold.

"Well, yeah. From some guy at the frat house. We just took that little ride and then I put it back and went back to the frat house. That was it. I haven't been on a motorcycle since."

"But I saw a book on caves in your room, Pruitt. That's how I figured out where to look for the bike."

"I was writing a report on caves. That's all that book was for. I didn't know where the bike was hidden. Didn't care. All I knew was, I wasn't the person attacking people, so I didn't really have anything to worry about. I heard what happened on the radio, and I knew you'd think it was me. So I just pretended it *was* me."

Echo turned on him. "You *sleaze*! You let me think it was you! You heard on the radio what had happened and you used that against me! You *threatened* me, you creep!"

"Welcome to the club." Deejay smiled thinly. "He really is a creep, isn't he?"

"You were never interested in me before," Pruitt whined. "You were only interested when you thought I had a motorcycle."

Echo stared at him. "But the boots, the bike . . ."

"He bought the boots in high school," Deejay said coldly. "Went through a brief phase when he thought being a biker might make him cool. It didn't, and he gave up on the idea. But he kept the leather stuff and the helmet. Got fired at the bike shop, though. Who wants a clerk who kills people? Too bad. He liked the shop, thought the people there were cool, especially my brother Ross."

The bike shop. That registered. "You were the clerk?" Echo asked Pruitt. "You were the one who screwed up Ross's bike?"

"It was an accident," Pruitt said.

"So the judge said," Deejay said coldly. To Echo, she said, "I don't have tennis elbow,

Echo. I never did. It's my legs that need that whirlpool, not my arms. They haven't been the same since the accident, and it nearly killed me every single time I had to climb on this bike, I was in so much pain. But I had to do it. He got off scot-free, and no one was willing to punish him except me."

"But . . . I found Pruitt's motorcycle license in the cave, just now."

Deejay smiled coldly. "It is *so* easy to doctor a license. That license used to be Ross's. I just took a picture of Pruitt right after I got to campus and had it laminated to the license. Changed a few dates. I put the license where I knew you'd find it, thinking you'd take it to the police. Then, when I thought you had a thing for him, I decided I'd have to forget the whole idea and just kill him myself. I was following you tonight, thinking I'd catch the two of you together. Kill two birds with one stone, as they say. When I saw you heading for the cave alone, I called Pruitt, told him I knew he was the Mad Biker and said he should meet me here, on the bridge. Of course," she added, her voice silky-smooth, "you have to die, too, Echo. You're too much a part of this now. But that's okay. I can deal with both of you at the same time."

"It was a mistake," Pruitt began to babble, "just a mistake. I liked Ross, I never intended for anything bad to happen to him, it wasn't my fault . . ."

"*That's* why you looked so shocked when I pretended my brother's name was Ross," Echo cried. "It was because it reminded you of what you'd done to Deejay and her brother."

"He did it on purpose," Deejay said. "I've always thought that." To Pruitt, she said, "You were jealous of him. He had everything you didn't, friends, a good job, a family that loved him. You don't have any of that."

"No," Pruitt moaned, "it's not true."

Using the railing as a prop, Echo pulled herself to her feet. "You blackmailed me," she accused, "when you knew the whole time that you weren't on that bike, except for that first ride. You let me think you would *kill* me!"

"I'm sorry! I'm sorry, I'm sorry! I couldn't help it. You were so pretty, and I saw my chance to be like everybody else, all those guys dating gorgeous girls. And it was fun telling someone else what to do for a change," Pruitt added petulantly. "I've been doing what other people told me to all of my life."

"No one told you to put that defective part on my brother's bike," Deejay said harshly.

"Echo, you have to stop her," Pruitt begged. "You can't let her kill me. It's not right. The judge said it wasn't my fault."

"Because of your father!" Deejay's words were scornful. "That judge knew you were guilty, just as I and my family did. But he wasn't willing to cross your very important father who contributed big bucks to the honorable judge's campaign. I know because I checked."

"I don't understand," Echo said, even as her eyes were glancing around the floor of the bridge, trying to locate the hole she had nearly fallen into on her way over. "Deejay, you were *alone* when you pushed that Miata off the cliff, and when you killed Gabriella Stone. I wasn't on that bike then. I couldn't have testified against Pruitt. Why did you do that?"

"To build a better case against him. I wanted you to ride with me, but I couldn't find you. Anyway, it didn't matter by then. At least, I thought it didn't. You *thought* it was Pruitt on the bike the whole time. I was sure that sooner or later, you'd turn him in. All I was doing was making sure he didn't go free again. Murder seemed the best way to do that. I almost went crazy when you still didn't blow the whistle on him."

"I didn't have any proof. But Deejay . . . you *killed* people!"

"So did he. Don't forget that, Echo."

"That's why you pushed me to date Pruitt," Echo said, her eyes finally locating the hole in the floor of the bridge. It was behind her, to her left. "You *wanted* people to see me on campus with him, so they would believe me when I told what he'd done. What I *thought* he'd done. But at the tennis match that day, you acted like you'd changed your mind. Why?"

"I thought you'd fallen for him. Hard to believe, but that was what it looked like. That ruined everything. I figured you'd never testify against him now. So I had to take matters into my own hands."

Echo fought to make sense of it all. "You took everything out of the cave after I found it? Why? Didn't you want the police to have the bike?"

"Not then. Too soon. You weren't supposed to find it so quickly, Echo. I underestimated you. I didn't have a strong enough case against Pruitt yet. So I moved it all and then put it back. I knew the police would never look there twice."

Realizing she was talking to a cold-blooded killer, Echo chose her words carefully. "Pruitt knew he wasn't on that bike at Johnny's Place, Deejay. He knew someone else was. Didn't you think he'd just tell me that, and that would be the end of it?"

Deejay threw her head back and laughed loudly. "Oh, Echo. I *know* what kind of person Pruitt is! I knew he'd love picturing himself as the Mad Biker, and he'd love it even more if a pretty girl pictured him that way, too. No way would he punch a hole in that theory. And I was right, wasn't I?"

Pruitt's eyes were wide with terror. He didn't answer. Echo thought perhaps he couldn't speak, he was so frightened. She tried to feel sorry for him, and couldn't.

Now, so suddenly that the noise seemed to explode in Echo's ears, Deejay turned the key and the motorcycle's engine roared.

"Echo, don't let her do this!" Pruitt begged, pushing so hard against the bridge railing that it leaned slightly backward. "I didn't mean it, I know I shouldn't have lied, shouldn't have scared you like that, but it felt so good to finally be in charge, and I didn't think it would hurt anything."

"You weren't in *charge* of me, Pruitt." Echo addressed him with almost as much contempt as Deejay had. "You *terrified* me! There's a difference. And it *did* hurt. It hurt a lot."

"I'm sorry, I'm sorry." The bike roared. "Echo, *do* something! She's going to kill me."

Seeing him standing there, trembling violently, hearing him whine to the point of tears, Echo had a hard time connecting him to the threatening, swaggering bully she'd known as Aaron Pruitt, the person who had made her life so miserable. She felt a raw, savage impulse to make him pay for what he had done to her. No punishment could be too severe, could it?

But then Deejay gunned the engine, fixed her dark eyes on him and tightened her mouth, and Echo knew that she couldn't stand the thought of one more death. Not even Pruitt's. "Deejay, you can't do this," she called over the engine's roar. "I know you've been through hell, but you can't kill him! Can't we just talk about it?"

"So, talk," Deejay said. And then she stomped down hard on the pedal and twisted the handlebars and the motorcycle raced across the bridge and slammed into Pruitt, flinging him up into the air, over the railing, and down into the cold, rushing water below.

He never even screamed.

Chapter 22

The force of the collision between Pruitt against the metal railing was strong enough to knock Deejay backwards, off the bike. She slid to the floor with a surprised look on her face. The bike bounced backward, too, then veered off to the side to land at Echo's feet. Seizing the opportunity, Echo reached down and yanked it upright. The motor was still running. She jumped on the seat, clutched the handlebars, her eyes never leaving Deejay for a second.

Deejay shook her head groggily, then got to her feet, one hand on the railing for support. "What do you think you're doing, Echo? That's my bike. It used to be Pruitt's, of course," she smiled a half-smile, "but I bought it, and for your information, it's still registered in his name. He didn't know that, of course. Thought he was completely rid of it. But I never changed the title when I bought it. And I used my mother's maiden name to buy it, just as I'm using it here at college, so he wouldn't know it was me. Ross's sister."

"You killed him," Echo whispered.

Deejay shrugged. "He had it coming. Should have done it long ago instead of coming up with this scheme that you blew all to hell. I've wanted to kill him ever since the accident. But I knew that if I did it, the police would investigate, and I'd be the very first person they'd suspect. Pruitt deserved to die, so why should I be punished for it? Justice, that's all it was. Justice. As far as I'm concerned, the idiot just fell off the bridge. Shouldn't have been out here in the middle of the night, especially in this fog."

"You killed him," Echo repeated dully. "Cold-blooded murder, that's what that was. Just like you killed Polk and Nancy and Gabriella. How can you say that Pruitt is worse than you? At least what he did *could* have been accidental. But not what *you* did. There wasn't anything accidental about any of those deaths."

Deejay stood up, her face twisted with rage. "Do you *know* what he did to you?" she screamed. "The only reason he knew anything about those first few incidents with the bike was because he'd heard about them on the radio. But when you went to him and told him you thought he was this mad, ferocious biker, he *loved* that idea. It was what he'd always wanted. So he pretended he'd actually been there. He saw an opportunity to make you dance a jig and he took it. He took it in a *big* way. You should *hate* him for that."

Frightened by the raw rage in Deejay's face and still in shock over Pruitt's death, Echo began backing away, mindful of the hole in the floor behind her. "I do! I . . . did. Hate him. And I don't blame you for hating him, after what he did to you. To your brother. But you still didn't have the right to kill him. Nobody has that right. Nobody."

She remembered the tape then. *Deejay's* tape. It was Deejay who'd been out for revenge, not Pruitt. And the tape wasn't one of the things Echo was supposed to have found. The books with Echo's name in them, yes, Deejay had clearly planted those in the cave. And the fake license. But the tape had been better hidden because it was the one thing Deejay wanted to keep for herself. That first night in the cave, Deejay couldn't have known that Echo was hiding in the crevasse while Deejay went insane with rage. So she wouldn't have expected Echo to know that opening was there, or to look inside it.

I have the bike, Echo thought, gripping the handlebars tightly, and I have the tape. That's enough. I can take them both to the police. They won't believe me at first, but when they hear the tape, they'll know I'm telling the truth. They will find Deejay and put her away where she can't hurt anyone else ever again.

And while she was thinking all of that, Deejay made a sudden end run around her. When Echo looked up, Deejay was standing between the bike and the exit from the bridge. "You're not going to get past me," she shouted over the engine's sputtering. "That's *my* bike! I want it. Give it to me!"

"Get out of my way!" Echo shouted back. "I'm leaving, and you can't stop me. You can't run me down the way you did Pruitt. *I'm* on the bike now. I'm the one with the power, not you."

Deejay waved her arms in dismissal. "You don't know the first thing about power *or* that bike! You couldn't steer around me in a million years, and you'd never have the guts to hit me. I *want* that bike, Echo."

Echo knew what she was up against. Deejay had no conscience. Not anymore.

But the bike was huge. If it was going fast enough, speeding as fast as it would go, the trip across the rest of the bridge would only take a second or two. And didn't Deejay know better than anyone the power of a motorcycle the size of this one? Desperate or not, would she really be foolish enough to try to stop it?

I have no choice, Echo told herself. Terrified that she wouldn't be able to steer the huge machine accurately enough to avoid the gaping hole in the floorboards up ahead, she revved the acelerator and the bike shot ahead.

For just one hopeful second, she thought she was going to speed by Deejay so fast she would leave her behind in the fog like a vapor trail.

But there was the hole, yawning wide and open. Echo had to veer around it, and when she did, Deejay seized the moment and leapt for the handlebars.

She misjudged the distance by a millimeter. The bike sideswiped her, knocking her sideways. She slipped and fell, at an angle, into the ragged opening in the floor of the bridge.

At the very last second, her right arm flew out and clutched the jagged end of a rotting board. It creaked ominously as her body weight pulled at it, but it held.

Deejay hung by one hand high above the cold, deep river.

Chapter 23

Echo yanked the bike to a screeching halt. She jumped off, lay it on its side, rushed over to the hole.

"Help me," Deejay whispered. "Echo, help me."

The floorboards groaned.

She is a murderer, Echo told herself, cautiously kneeling beside the gaping hole. A cold-blooded murderer. She's insane. If you try to pull her up, this whole part of the bridge could cave in. You'd both die in that water down there.

She could hear the river gurgling, bubbling, as if it were excited at the prospect of two more victims following Pruitt.

"Please, Echo, please," Deejay pled. "Don't let me fall!"

"If I pull you up," she told Deejay even as

she leaned precariously close to the hole, "you'll kill me."

"No, no, I won't. Not if you help me. I never wanted to hurt you, Echo, it was Pruitt, only Pruitt."

The board Deejay was holding bent lower, sending out an agonized squeal. Deejay gasped.

"You have to go to the police, Deejay," Echo said shakily, lying flat on her stomach on the wet floor of the bridge. "You have to tell them the truth."

"I will, I will! I promise! Just get me up, get me up, Echo, *please!*"

She will kill me the instant she's safe, Echo thought with conviction.

But she didn't have it in her to let Deejay fall.

Reaching behind her, she yanked the heavy helmet off the bike's handlebars, looped the strap around her right arm and pulled it up to her shoulder. It was the only thing mildly resembling a weapon she had left. Then she dropped her arms into the hole and instructed Deejay to grab them.

The boards screamed in anger the whole time Echo was slowly, painstakingly inching her way backward on the slippery, wet floor of the bridge with Deejay clinging to her arms. The former tennis player was heavier than

Echo, and the strain on Echo's back and shoulders was unbearable.

After what seemed to Echo like hours, the last of Deejay, her legs and feet, came up out of the hole and flopped limply next to an exhausted Echo. The helmet was prodding her chest painfully, and she reached over to slide the strap down and off her arm. Then she lay on her back on the cool, wet floor of the bridge and struggled to get her strength back.

They lay there silently for a long time, breathing hard, the fog and the dampness of the bridge's surface seeping into their clothes, chilling them to the bone.

Finally, Echo turned her head, to find herself staring straight into Deejay's eyes.

Deejay was smiling without warmth. "You are such an utter fool, Echo." The arm that came up from beside her then was holding the baseball bat. She began to raise it over Echo's head. Her eyes were tiny slits of hatred. "Such a fool."

"No. I'm not." Echo's fingers closed around the solid, hard plastic helmet, and she brought it up and around, slamming it against Deejay's temple.

The baseball bat fell harmlessly to the bridge surface and rolled away.

Echo didn't get up right away.

When she did, she walked slowly, painfully, over to the baseball bat, picked it up and tossed it over the railing. It made a satisfying splash when it hit the water.

Then she went back and picked up the helmet and put it on, looking at an unconscious Deejay. She returned to the motorcycle, lifted it upright, climbed on, and started the engine. The roar exploded into the fog like the cry of a wild animal.

Patting her pocket once to make sure the tape of Deejay's voice telling all was still there, Echo rode the bike off the bridge, back to campus.

She sat on the bike well, her shoulders back, her head high.

Epilogue

Finals over, they sat on the low stone wall around the fountain on the Commons and let the fine, cool spray relieve the heat of the day. Echo was wearing the pretty white dress she had put back on the rack when she went shopping with Deejay at the mall, and Liam had an arm casually draped around her shoulders. Marilyn and Ruthanne, fresh from the whirlpool, finger-combed their hair.

"I can't believe you thought I had an aunt named Ross," Marilyn said, smiling at Echo. "Why would anyone name a girl Ross?"

"Why would anyone name a girl Echo?" Echo responded. But she returned the smile. "You really should do something about your penmanship, Marilyn. If that last letter on your aunt's name had looked like the 'e' it was supposed to be instead of an 's,' I would have known it was 'Rose.' "

"True. But to tell you the truth, Echo, I'm kind of flattered that you thought the Mad Biker could be me, even for a little while."

"Marilyn!" Ruthanne exclaimed. "Are you serious? That's disgusting! Deejay was seriously sick in the head. She's going to be in an institution for the rest of her life."

"I know. I didn't say I wanted to *be* her. Or even be *like* her. I know she's sick. It's just that most people who know me could never imagine me riding a motorcycle in the first place, and of course I couldn't, with my legs the way they are from the fire. People see me as someone shy and quiet and probably afraid of my own shadow. But Echo could picture me on that bike, so maybe she doesn't see me that way."

"I don't think you're afraid of anything," Echo said matter-of-factly. "How many other people do I know who saved their entire family from dying in a house fire, burning themselves seriously in the process? That's not the profile of a coward, Marilyn."

"Well, you saved Deejay. You could have just let her fall into the river. Lots of people would have, Echo."

"I would have," Liam said, tilting his head back to let the sun shine on his face. "I most certainly would have. After what she did . . ."

"No, you wouldn't have," Echo contradicted. "You would have wanted to. But you'd have pulled her up out of there just like I did. So would Marilyn. You, too, Ruthanne."

Ruthanne lifted a skeptical eyebrow.

"If I didn't know that about all of you," Echo added, "I wouldn't be sitting here with you now. Anyone who would have let Deejay drop to her death would be as bad as she was."

"That's true," Liam agreed grudgingly.

"We all know I am an antisocial pain in the neck who doesn't make friends easily," Echo said, beginning to smile. "The only reason I have made an exception in your cases is because you are the only people on campus who know exactly what happened. You could blackmail me, threaten to tell everyone on campus all about how I was involved with Pruitt against my will. So I have to be very, very nice to all of you."

Ruthanne was shocked again. "Echo! How can you joke about blackmail after what Pruitt did to you?"

Echo shrugged. "I figure I have two choices here, Ruthanne. I can either laugh about it now that it's all over and I'm being allowed to stay in school as long as I do nine zillion hours of community service, or I can spend the rest of my life crying about it and jumping every time

I hear the roar of a motorcycle. Pruitt is dead, Deejay's safe inside a hospital she can't get out of, and I'm here. I'm alive and well, and in the company of friends. What's not to laugh about?"

Twenty minutes later when a motorcycle's engine roared past campus on the highway and Echo instinctively jumped so high she almost fell into the fountain, she laughed as loudly as anyone else.

About the Author

"Writing tales of horror makes it hard to convince people that I'm a nice, gentle person," says **Diane Hoh**.

"So what's a nice woman like me doing scaring people?"

"Discovering the fearful side of life: what makes the heart pound, the adrenaline flow, the breath catch in the throat. And hoping always that the reader is having a frightfully good time, too."

Diane Hoh grew up in Warren, Pennsylvania. Since then, she has lived in New York, Colorado, and North Carolina, before settling in Austin, Texas. "Reading and writing take up most of my life," says Hoh, "along with family, music, and gardening." Her other horror novels include *Funhouse*, *The Accident*, *The Invitation*, *The Fever*, and *The Train*.

He just keeps talking and talking and talking. His mouth flaps open and shut, open and shut, like that dumb goldfish I had when I was eight instead of the puppy I really wanted. Every time I think he's finally going to shut up and let me talk, he opens his mouth again.

He never lets me talk. Loves the sound of his own voice too much. But he's getting paid to listen, isn't he? Isn't that what a shrink is supposed to do?

"Let me talk!" I scream at him, and he looks up at me like I've lost my mind.

Oh, that's funny. That's really funny. Of course I've lost my mind, or I wouldn't be in this stupid office in the first place with the eminent Dr. Milton Leo, would I?

"Now, now," he says, "there's no need to shout." He lays aside his notebook, sits up straighter in his chair, and I can see something in his eyes that I've never seen before.

Fear.

He's *afraid of* me! *What a rush! Mr.-I-Am-Un-Control-Here-At-All-Times is not so cool now, is he? All because of one tiny little shout.*

I like the effect so much, I decide to shout some more. And once I start, I can't stop. I shout and I shout. I tell him he's a stupid jerk who doesn't know the first thing about psychiatry, that he's the one who needs the shrink, not me. I shout that if he tells me one more time I have to take responsibility for my own actions, I'm going to hit him with that big gold lamp on the table beside his left elbow.

And then that's what I do.

I don't mean to. It's not something I think about ahead of time. But the lamp is sitting right there beside him and it looks so heavy and so solid and I can't resist it.

He was supposed to help me, and he didn't.

I think the reason he doesn't move out of the way in time is he can't believe it's happening. Not to him. That's what I see in his face as I lunge for the lamp, grab it off the table and bring it down hard on the left side of his head. I see astonishment in those dark, cold eyes behind the glasses. Not me, he's thinking.

So much blood. I expected ice-water to flow from that coldhearted creep, but it's blood, all right.

I feel bad for Tanner. He's her father, after all. I guess they didn't get along that great, but still . . . Tanner was always nice to me.

But, he made me do it! Sitting there so smug, so pompous, passing judgment on me. Shrinks aren't supposed to pass judgment. Then he had to go and bring up that nasty business two years ago. That wasn't my fault, either, but he made it sound like it was.

I need to think, but my head aches really bad.

He never even screamed. I know he told people that I wasn't violent, I saw one of the reports he signed. I'll bet he was sorry he ever wrote that when he saw that lamp coming at him.

Think, think . . .

This is the worst. I can't hide this. No way. His secretary has gone home. She never saw me come in. And I didn't have an appointment, just dropped in on the off chance that he'd see me, so no one knows I was here except him and me. And neither one of us is going to tell.

But the police will check out his patients and they'll find out about two years ago and they'll come looking for me. They'll put me away again.

I can't go back to that place. I won't.

Don't panic, panic is the worst thing. It makes the headaches unbearable.

Think, think . . .

There has to be a way.

They're not taking me back there. I'll do anything to stay out of that place.

Anything.

The first thing is, to get out of here. But how far can I go in this storm? The roads might be washed out.

I have to find a place to hide.

Somewhere where no one would think to look for me . . .

I think I know just the place . . .

THRILLERS